It's Always My Fault

It's Always My Fault

and Other Short Stories

L.D. Zane

Pretzel City Press

Reading, PA

It's Always My Fault Copyright © 2020 by L.D. Zane. All Rights Reserved.

Cover photography by Angela Cremer, AJC Photography.

Contents

	Dedications	vii
	Foreword	ix
	Stories by Beverage	xi
1.	It's Always My Fault	1
2.	Driving Lessons	13
3.	It Happened Over Coffee…and a Bagel	19
4.	Benjamin Stahlman, Scholar	39
5.	Wooden Statements	51
6.	The Box	53
7.	Separated at Birth	57
8.	I Thought Death Would Be Fun	73
9.	As If	97
10.	Done with Crazy	111
11.	Where's the Cow?	117
12.	Solomon's Shadow	119
13.	Combustible	127

14.	Kintsugi	*135*
	Publishing Credits	*155*

Dedications

To my beloved father, Louis. A gentle man of quiet intellect: 1916–1984.
A child of the Depression; a young man who helped save the world from tyranny; a father who saved me from myself.

To my editor and friend, Marian Wolbers, who believed in me when I doubted myself.
And without whose encouragement, and guidance, these stories and this anthology would not have seen the light of day.

Foreword

Here is a writer who patrols the DMZ of life, alternately fearless and fearful, ever ruthlessly honest. His characters echo and emerge from the American landscape he's intimately familiar with—from the family home to city streets to Vietnam. They grab the reader by the arm, pulling them into skirmishes and battles of relationships, goals, encounters, and all of the coping that men and women and children seem to do when they experience—often in hindsight—love missing, love lost, and love gained.

As edgy, even combative, as some of L.D. Zane's characters are, we like them. Often they become ensnared in the bitter taste of reality; frequently, we can count on them for an emergence of humility, a tender core, a turn of the heart, a window to epiphany, as these beloved figures come around to meet themselves.

In "Where's the Cow?" and "Kintsugi," for example, we are both startled and gratified as the characters revisit the past but decide to freshly embrace life despite its messiness and sorrow. In "The Box," we enjoy L.D. Zane's backhanded humor and sardonic disdain for the silliness of the American workplace. Misguided managerial efforts, at coddling workers through a year-end reward system, are thwarted by two savvy workers who believe the box to be more beautiful than its contents.

It's a fact that a DMZ, while deserted, is no desert but is instead lush: its land that remains protected, undisturbed, though bristling on either side as warring factions keep watch. Within that lush land thrives the literary imagination of L.D. Zane, allowing for characters and plots to act, and talk, and come full circle in safety and beauty. Perhaps that's why we like these stories. The characters are clearly separate from us, and we know it. But on some level, by the end of each story, we recognize baldly that *they are us*. And we thank the author for taking up the sword and penning them for us to move past the emotional walls that we have unwittingly set up inside ourselves—not remembering we did that, until a story moves us inside, shifting the borders of head and heart.

It has been my distinct pleasure and honor to witness and be inspired by the literary journey of L.D. Zane. As he continues to work his pen, self-mustered into the art of storytelling, this author—I predict—will continue to hike his way, eyes and ears alert, along sharp blades of tall grass, revealing rich truths as he forges onward.

–Marian Frances Wolbers
April 2020

Stories by Beverage

A companion tongue-in-cheek list of imbibing suggestions for readers.

It's Always My Fault – **Beer** (Out of the bottle, and preferably not of the "light" variety)
Driving Lessons – **Harvey Wallbanger**
It Happened Over Coffee…and a Bagel – **Manhattan**
Benjamin Stahlman, Scholar – **Merlot** (Out of a box)
Wooden Statements – **Hard Apple Cider**
The Box – **Gin and Tonic**
Separated at Birth – **Dirty Martini**
I Thought Death Would Be Fun – **White Russian**
As If – **Sloe Gin**
Done with Crazy – **Irish Coffee**
Where's the Cow? – **Boone's Farm** (Your choice of flavor)
Solomon's Shadow – **Vodka**
Combustible – **Irish or Scotch Whiskey** (Pick your poison)
Kintsugi – **Sake**

1

It's Always My Fault

"Are you Heller? Albert Jackson Heller?"

I was used to being questioned by the police. If it wasn't for the constant truancy, fighting, or alleged petty crimes, then it was for some car that had gone missing somewhere within the city limits. But I learned how *not* to answer them.

"You know who I am, Officer Bolton, as would anyone who's been on the force more than a week. What about it?" I was already bored with the conversation.

He pointed to the suit next to him. "This is Detective Robinson."

I smiled and thought, *Yeah. Like no one would know* he's *a cop.* "How may I be of assistance to two of this fair city's finest?"

The detective wasted no time setting the tone of the meeting. "Now that we've established who the fuck you are, we can either have a friendly chat here and now, or we can have a not-so-friendly chat in my office. Choose wisely, Heller."

When will this shit end? But I already knew the answer. I took a swig of my beer and put it down, lit another Camel, and sat on top of the splintered, weather-beaten, wood picnic table. It was as worn as my jeans. *This table looks and feels like my life.*

Officer Bolton slapped the cigarette out of my mouth with his left hand and then smashed my beer bottle with his baton and said, "You shouldn't be smoking, asshole. It's bad for your health. And the legal age for consuming alcohol is twenty-one. You're only eighteen. I should run you in for underage drinking." *But you won't, Bolton, because you've never done it before. Why are you playing the hard-ass cop?*

Detective Robinson casually lit up a Lucky Strike and said, "Now, where were we, Heller?" and paused. "Ah yes, I remember. You were deciding where you wanted to chat." He opened his hands in a questioning manner and cocked his head like the RCA dog.

"Well, it is Saturday, and movie night," I said. Those were the days when twice a month, during the summer—weather permitting—the city playgrounds would show an open-air movie on a large screen. The Recreation Department reasoned it was a good way to keep us street urchins occupied so we wouldn't be roaming the streets looking for targets of opportunity. It worked—sort of. Most of the older kids—like me—took advantage of the opportunity to find a quiet spot behind the rec building to get drunk, or laid, or both.

"And they're going to be showing *Bullitt* in about an hour. How appropriate. Don't you think so, Officers?" Without looking at him, Detective Robinson grabbed Officer Bolton's right arm with his left hand. *Thank God for restraint.*

Detective Robinson decided to play the good cop. "Why don't you take a seat on the bench, on the opposite side. I'll just sit on this side, and then we can have that friendly chat and get you back in time for the movie."

He added, "You don't want to miss it, Heller. I've seen that flick. It's a real thriller."

The detective turned his head toward Officer Bolton. "Officer Bolton. Would you be good enough to stand back a few feet?"

"And holster your baton," I chimed in.

"And holster your baton, Officer. No need for violence." The detective looked at me. "Right, Heller?" Detective Robinson sat and grabbed a beer from my six-pack and handed it to me, and then took one for himself. "You don't mind if I help myself? I could use a cold one after today."

"Not at all, Detective," I said with a smirk. "But why this sudden act of generosity?"

"Well, although I agree with Officer Bolton's assessment of the law, he was a bit hasty in his reaction. And I just want you to be more...at ease."

"Thanks, Detective. And are you going to offer one to Officer Bolton?"

"No. He's on duty."

"And you're not?" I asked, laughing.

"I am. But rank has its privileges," he said, not cracking a smile. "Smoke if you want. I will."

I looked at Officer Bolton and, with a shit-eating grin, said, "Only if Officer Bolton approves."

Officer Bolton just looked straight ahead and then tapped his baton with his fingertips.

"I'll take that as a 'yes.'" I lit up another cigarette. There was an awkward moment of silence and stares all around. So, I took the initiative. "What's on your mind, Detective?"

"Did you read today's newspaper?"

"I didn't, Detective. I was too busy getting my affairs in order before I leave for college."

"That's right! I heard you were accepted at some fancy Ivy League school, Heller. Part of the arrangement your Jew lawyer made with the judge. Congratulations."

I felt slighted. *Where were the congratulations when I graduated from high school, or the numerous stints in reform school?*

I started stealing cars when I was sixteen, but was treated as a juvie when caught. That summer I boosted another one. Of course I was caught. The difference was that I was now eighteen and would be treated as an adult.

My attorney struck a deal with the judge—the very same one who had dealt with me as a juvenile: If I graduated from a four-year college, or served honorably for four years in the military, my sealed record would be expunged. It was either that or four years in the county prison. I briefly thought about taking the prison option. It was, after all, the height of the Vietnam War, and I didn't have a death wish. But the prospect of sharing a cell for four years with "Big Bob" wasn't appealing either. I chose college and was accepted because of my attorney's influence. He never mentioned my youthful indiscretions.

"That's correct, Detective. And thank you for your well wishes. But there's no need to bring my attorney's religion into this."

"What-the-fuck-ever, Heller. You belong behind bars. But the judge is still the judge." He took a long swig of his beer, finishing off the bottle, and then finished his smoke. "Don't mind if I do," he then added, helping himself to another beer.

"Want one of my smokes too, Detective?" I asked.

He squared his look on me and said, "You really should keep your fucking mouth shut, Heller, other than when you're answering my questions. Do I need to reintroduce you to Officer Bolton?" Officer Bolton wrapped his right hand around the handle of the baton and took two steps forward.

I looked up at Officer Bolton, and he looked at me. Detective Robinson took a few gulps of his beer and lit yet another cigarette. "No. I'm good. Please continue, Detective. What was in *The Daily Rag* that caught your attention?"

"Funny you should ask. It seems that the Dutch Restaurant burned to the ground last night."

"Sorry to hear that," I said. "Fine eating establishment."

"What do you know about it?"

"The fire, or the dining experience at the Dutch Restaurant?"

"The fire, Heller. What do you know about it?"

"I don't know shit about it. And why would you ask me about a fire, Detective?"

"Because I understand, Heller, that you worked there briefly—for about two weeks, if I'm correct—and were fired for stealing money two days ago. Now that didn't surprise me."

"Which part, Detective?"

"What?"

"Which part didn't surprise you? My getting fired, or allegedly stealing the money? Which part?"

The detective was now clearly agitated. "Just answer the question, Heller. Did you work there or not, and were you fired for stealing money?"

It sounded more like a statement of fact than a question. But for the sake of the conversation, I answered, "You wouldn't ask any question you didn't already know the answer to. But yeah, I worked there, Detective. I was just trying to earn some extra cash before going to college."

"What? Your grandfather isn't paying you well enough?"

My grandfather did pay me well enough. My best friend Mikey and I had worked for my Russian-born, bookie grandfather since we were ten years old. We became his collection agency at sixteen. I took the restaurant job to appease the judge and my parents, and they knew it. I made more in one day with my grandfather than I did in two weeks at that lousy restaurant. They probably knew that too.

"I don't know what you're talking about. As I said, I was just trying to put aside a few more bucks for school."

"Why would you need the extra money, Heller? I thought the college was giving you a free ride—hardship case and all."

A hardship case I am. But money was what the college was thinking of. "They are, but it doesn't include money for beer, cigarettes, and whores."

The detective just shook his head in disbelief. Then he continued: "Is that why you stole the money?"

"I didn't steal shit. What's your beef?"

"My beef is that you were fired, for *allegedly* stealing money, and that looks like a motive for you to torch the place."

"Fuck you, Detective!" Surprisingly, the detective didn't react. I fully expected Officer Goon to rap me across the mouth with his stick. But he didn't. So I continued. "I was a busboy and the waitresses were supposed to split their tips with me. All of them did, except one bitch who decided she wasn't going to play by the same rules as the others. I complained to the manager, but he just laughed and said, 'Suck it up, convict!'"

"And that's when you stole the money?"

"I already told you, Detective, I stole nothing. Take the shit out of your ears."

He leaned into me. "One more smart-ass remark like that, Heller, and I'm going to have Officer Bolton rip off your head. Then I'm going to take the shit from my ears and shove it down your neck!"

It wouldn't have been the first time someone tried to take off my head. And I have over a dozen stitches on the left side of my skull to prove it. That was the result of a baseball bat wielded by a deadbeat customer I was trying to collect from.

We glared at each other for a few moments. Then he asked, matter-of-factly, "So why would they fire you if you didn't steal the money?"

"It was my last night. I asked the waitress in question, again, for the money she owed me for the past two weeks. I figured it was about a hundred bucks or so. The bitch just walked away. So at the end of the evening, I went to her tip jar and took what was in it. I just took what was rightfully mine, Detective. Simple as that."

"And how much was that?"

"Fifty bucks. That's it. A lousy fifty dollars. That's all she had."

"What happened then?"

"She saw me take the money and told me to put it back. I told her to go fuck herself—which, given her looks, was probably the only way she was going to get any." Officer Bolton turned away. He strained not to laugh. Detective Robinson lowered his head. But I saw him crack an ever-so-slight smile.

"Then she ratted me out to the manager. He came over and told me to give him the money. I told him the same thing I told her. He said he was going to call the cops and that I shouldn't go anywhere."

"Did you wait?"

"For who?"

"The police, dipshit. Did you wait for the police?"

"Yes, I did. I poured myself a cup of coffee, sat down and ate a ham sandwich I made, and then had a piece of apple pie for dessert while I waited for the police."

I paused, expecting a comment. None came.

"What the fuck do you think I did, Detective? I split. So, are you here to arrest me for taking what was mine?"

"No. I don't give a shit about the money, Heller. But I do give a shit about the fire, and your possible involvement."

"I had nothing to do with the fire! The place was a fire trap. Everyone knew it. I'm amazed it didn't burn down long ago. Why don't you question the owner about how the fire started?"

"Why would I do that?"

"Because business has been slow for years. Everyone knew that too. Maybe he lit it up to get the insurance money."

"That crossed our minds, and the investigation is still ongoing. But given your rap sheet—and the firing—you seemed a likely suspect."

"Yeah," I said, and sighed, "it's always my fault." *When will this shit end?* "No matter what happens in or around the city, you guys eye me. It's true—I wouldn't have pissed on the fire to put it out. And had I known about it, I probably would have used the money I took from that shit hole to buy hot dogs and marshmallows, and had a good ol'-fashioned cookout. But I had nothing to do with it. NOTHING!"

"Excuse me while I wipe the tears from my eyes, Heller. You always bring this shit down on yourself with your criminal behavior. And just for the record—where were you last night?"

"I was playing cards with my grandfather right here at the playground. Go ask him."

The detective rolled his eyes. "And I'm sure *he'll* tell me the truth." He glanced over his shoulder at Officer Bolton, then looked back at me. "You know," he said with a big grin, "I think it's time you took a ride with us," and winked.

A "ride" didn't necessarily mean downtown to police headquarters. Many times it meant you were going to be taken to an isolated location, and if the police didn't get the right answers, you were beaten to within an inch of your life. Jail was usually safer. The phrase "police brutality" wasn't yet part of the lexicon—at least not when referring to what happened to guys like me. It was just considered "restraining an uncooperative detainee."

"Officer Bolton. Place Heller under arrest for the arson of the Dutch Restaurant."

Then suddenly, out of nowhere, as the playground moved from dusk to dark, there he was—my grandfather, right on cue. *The man always had impeccable timing.*

He strode forward with three of his associates in tow—the same three men he had played cards with for as long as I can remember. "What's going on, Officers?" he said, in his now-faint Russian accent.

Detective Robinson snapped back, "None of your business, pops."

"Everything that happens around here is my business, Detective," my grandfather responded coolly.

The detective turned toward the officer. "Officer Bolton. Get on with it!"

My grandfather and his associates moved between me and Officer Bolton.

As a young man, my grandfather had been a bare-knuckled prizefighter. He stood six-three. Even in his seventies he still had an athletic build, and no one challenged him. He was his own sole authority, and he was the king. "You're not taking my grandson anywhere, gentlemen."

I smiled inwardly. *At least my grandfather loves me. Then, again, he always did protect his investments.*

"Step back, old man," said Detective Robinson, "or I'll have you arrested for interfering with a police officer's official duties."

"That won't happen, Detective. Do you know who I am?"

"Yeah. You're Solomon Jackson, the alleged bookie king of my city. So what?"

"How long have you been on the force, Detective?"

"About a year. What about it?"

"And you, Officer?"

"Fifteen years. You know that, Sol. And we don't want any trouble here. Just step aside. Please?"

"You're pretty close to retirement, Bolton. Is that right?"

"Yeah. I have five more years and then I intend to retire."

"Congratulations. You've served this city well. But if either of you ever hope to see your retirement, I suggest *you* step aside."

Detective Robinson shouted, "Bolton. Call for backup."

"Stay where you are, Bolton!" commanded my grandfather. And then he turned toward the detective. "And what exactly do you think backup will do, Detective?"

"They'll haul all of your criminal asses to jail."

"If you truly know who I am, Detective, then you must know that will never happen either."

"And why is that, you commie bastard?"

My grandfather showed no reaction to that comment. Instead, he explained in a measured tone, "Because half of the force does business with me," and turned toward Officer Bolton, "just as you do, Bolton, as do most of the judges. And the other half protects me. That's why, Detective. Now, I'm willing to forget this unfortunate incident," and again turned to Officer Bolton, "and that tidy sum of money you owe me, Bolton. Go find the real culprit of that tragic fire, and leave Jaks alone."

Without another word, my grandfather put his right arm around me. "Come, Jackson, the movie is about to start. I understand it's about a policeman just doing his best to perform his duties. How appropriate."

As we were walking away, my grandfather stopped and turned toward both Detective Robinson and Officer Bolton—who just stood there looking like two kids after they had been dressed down by the principal—and calmly proclaimed to the world: "And if either of you ever lay a hand on my grandson, or his friends, again, I will have them cut off and shoved up your asses, and the real police will find you floating facedown in the river. You will never see your retirement, *gentlemen,* except in Hell."

I wonder who he'd designate for that *job?*

And then, as a goodwill gesture, he said, "You can take the rest of the beer, Detective," and finally smiled.

Officer Bolton and Detective Robinson left as quietly as they arrived. They didn't take the beer. I went back and finished it—along with another six-pack—while I watched the movie. Detective Robinson was right. It was a real thriller.

Later that night, I drove to the smoldering carcass of the Dutch Restaurant. I was wrong when I told the detective I wouldn't have pissed on it.

2

Driving Lessons

"Your father taught me how to drive on this very road. And I had to learn on a stick shift," Gertrude proudly proclaimed, looking straight ahead while riding shotgun in Ian's car.

Ian had heard that proclamation countless times—every other Sunday, in fact, for years, when he and Gertrude traveled that road to visit Ian's son and granddaughter, her grandson and great granddaughter. Each time Ian would roll his eyes. Then, with as much enthusiasm as he could muster would say, "Really. Tell me about it." Ian always talked to the windshield.

He rarely used the title "Mom" when talking to his mother. Ian didn't like her, let alone love her. The feeling was mutual, but he still felt some obligation to cart her along whenever he would visit his son and granddaughter. Now in her nineties, and a widow for thirty years, Gertrude wasn't sure how many more visits were left, and neither was Ian. He never pondered that thought very long, being afraid in which direction his thoughts might take him.

She would drone on, sometimes for fifteen minutes, sometimes longer, but the story was always the same. The only difference was the length of her pauses as she searched for the right words, or perhaps thought about the relationship she'd had with her husband.

"He was always so patient," Gertrude would say in a halting, slightly haughty voice, "especially when I was learning how to start from a dead stop going up a hill, or how to slow the car going downhill, by shifting into a lower gear instead of using the brakes." The only time she would look over at Ian was when she got to this line: "Your father would always touch my hand and say, 'You're doing great, Gertrude.'" Ian never took his eyes off the road.

She would continue with a smile and a distinct pride in her voice: "I was the very first person who took the driving test on the State Police course, and I passed it on the very first try. I owed that success to your father—his knowledge, his patience, his gentle but commanding touch. There was even an article in the paper!"

"I know. I've seen and read the clipping," Ian said slightly above a mumble. It was becoming more difficult to hide his bored expression as he thought, exasperated, *How many more times do I need to hear this story? Our responses are always the same. It's like Groundhog Day.* He continued to address Gertrude: "It's the one you had laminated and sits next to dad's laminated obit, in the hutch." Ian asked himself, *But where are the articles of me serving in Vietnam, or how I was wounded and spent four hellish months in a military hospital in Hawaii learning how to walk again?* As far as Ian was concerned, there was only one article of value. "I would like that obit, if you don't mind," he said with a clipped tone.

Gertrude always responded in a taunting manner, her nose tilted slightly upwards, "Perhaps someday, Ian."

Then she would say no more, yet was still telling the story quietly in her head. Perhaps she just didn't want Ian to know that much about her relationship with his father or, then again, perhaps there was nothing more to tell.

But Ian thought he knew better from what he had witnessed as a child, then through adulthood, before his father's death—the looks his father got from other women when he entered a room and his quick glances of acknowledgment, or the longer-than-expected hugs and kisses women gave him without any resistance on his part, or the lack of a response from his father when Gertrude would say she loved him as he left the house for work, or that when offered the day shift at the post office, he chose to stay on grave-yard—that maybe she wasn't the love of his father's life. Gertrude felt differently. She always professed that his father was the first, and only, love of her life. Gertrude never dated another man after her husband's death, or removed her wedding ring.

A confession Gertrude made to Ian, on one occasion several years after his father's death, led Ian to believe that perhaps she knew more than what he thought, when she stated matter-of-factly: "I believe that had I died first, your father would probably have remarried within a year, or at very least, would have taken up with another woman—or women. And that's assuming he didn't leave me first." Ian wanted to retaliate to that revelation by saying, 'I believe you're right,' with an ear-to-ear-grin. But he held back, because he had no interest in continuing the conversation, as it now became apparent—to his great satisfaction—that Gertrude witnessed the same events. Instead, his only thought was, *Let sleeping dogs lie.*

Ian had his version of the truth about his father's true feelings toward Gertrude, and Gertrude had hers. Much to his dismay Ian couldn't confirm either, as that secret was locked in his father's grave and now inside Gertrude's head.

Two weeks passed.

The next time Ian stopped at Gertrude's house to pick her up for their Sunday journey, she was staring at some pictures of herself and her husband which hung on the living room wall. There were a few portraits: one of the two of them after their wedding, with Ian's father dressed in his Army uniform, and another taken on their fortieth wedding anniversary, which was about a year before he passed away. There were also various pictures of them dancing together at celebratory events. She turned to Ian, and with her wrinkled, left hand pointed and said commandingly, "Please remove these pictures, Ian—they're just collecting dust."

At first, Ian was shocked, hurt and angry, but hid it. He wasn't one to wear his heart on his sleeve: *How could she do this to my father?* he asked himself, and closed his eyes, shaking his head in disbelief. *Whatever his faults were as a husband, he more than made up as a father. He always stood between me and her when I got in trouble as a kid, and he was the only one who visited, or wrote or called me when I was recuperating in Hawaii. Not one lousy word from her. Not one. She never gave a shit about me and still doesn't. It's always been about her, or her fucking driving lessons.*

The shock quickly vanished, but not the hurt and anger. He was sobbing inside, still mourning his father as his thoughts rambled on: *I'm glad she's taking down these pictures. He was too good for her. I'm surprised he stayed with her as long as he did. She should have died first—at least then he would have had a shot at being happy. I don't ever want to see the two of them together again. Ever.* Ian stood bolt upright, and was resolute in his response to her request: "My pleasure."

As he took down the pictures, he still found himself fixated on the image of Gertrude's left hand when she pointed. Something was different. But what? Reality struck and Ian's eyes grew wide. He asked flatly, "Where's your wedding ring?"

It's Always My Fault

Gertrude reached into her right coat pocket and produced the ring, then went to the hutch and retrieved the laminated obit; a three-by-one-inch article. Ian stood motionless, a silent spectator not knowing what to expect. Gertrude walked back to Ian, opened his right hand and placed both objects on it. She looked squarely into Ian's clear, hazel eyes and spoke softly, but with a slightly aggrieved tone: "The obituary is for you. Give the ring to your granddaughter when the time is right. Perhaps she will have better luck than I did. Let's go."

Gertrude paused. "And, Ian…please take a different road."

3

It Happened Over Coffee...and a Bagel

As I waited for my order at Starbucks, someone from behind me said, "Avi. That's short for the Hebrew name Avraham. Are you Jewish?"

I turned to see who was speaking to me. He was a stocky young man sporting a beard, about five-ten, perhaps in his early twenties, and appeared to be Semitic.

"Yeah. It's short for Avraham, and I'm Jewish. What about it?"

Avi. My late parents—more precisely, my mother—thought sending me to Hebrew school during the school year (beginning when I turned eight) and to Brooklyn to study at a Chassidic yeshiva for one month during the summer break (until my Bar Mitzvah, at the age of thirteen) would thwart my juvenile delinquent behavior. It didn't.

But I always had a thirst for understanding how, and why, things were the way they were. The more I learned, the more questions I had. "Twenty-question Avi" was my nickname while attending religious schools. Surprisingly, I was a better student at the religious schools than I ever was at the secular ones. I never found my secular studies challenging.

Anyway, the Rabbis referred to me by my Hebrew name, Avraham ben Lazer—which translated to Avraham, the son of Lazer. It got shortened by others in my classes, from an early age, to just "Avi." It's come to be a term of endearment. And to this day, I have only allowed a select few to use the name. The stranger wasn't one of them.

"As-salām 'alaykum," is how he greeted me.

"That's Arabic. Are you an Arab?"

"Actually, Palestinian."

I glared at him for a moment, and then responded, "Same difference."

He smiled. "I beg to differ. But this is neither the time nor place for that discussion."

I continued the stare and said, "You can 'beg to differ' all you want. As far as I'm concerned, there's nothing to discuss." But to show I wasn't a complete boor, I responded to his greeting: "Wa 'alaykum as-salām."

I usually don't venture into Starbucks. The coffee is overpriced and overrated for my taste; they're always crowded; it's located on the wrong side of town—the affluent side, called The Hills; and most of the patrons—at least to me—are pretentious. Everyone is on their laptop or tablet. I have no idea what they're doing, nor do I care. The only reason I came this time was because I had one of their $30 gift cards, which I won in a contest at work, and I had some time to kill on my day off—two days before New Year's Eve day. I don't know why our company thinks going to Starbucks is a gift.

As I was standing in line looking over the menu of coffees, I became overwhelmed—and I'm not easily subjugated by fits of indecision. Not only were there two boards, but each selection had a calorie count and at least three sizes from which to choose.

There were two women in front of me agonizing over what to order. They finally settled on the type of coffee they wanted, but then anguished about the size in order to stay within their prescribed daily caloric intake. Finally, one of them said, "Oh...the hell with it. Who am I fooling? I stopped counting calories on Thanksgiving. I'm even going to get it with whipped cream!" The other agreed and they gleefully placed their orders.

Whatever happened to: "Coffee for here"?

I was up next and made it simple for the cashier: "Medium house blend and a toasted bagel with cream cheese."

"That's it? Just plain coffee? she said with condescension.

"Yeah. Just plain ol' coffee."

"Regular or decaf?"

"Regular. I like caffeine."

The inquisition continued. "What kind of bagel?"

"What kind do you have?"

She pointed to the menu, and said, "Everything, raisin or plain."

"Just a plain bagel," I responded.

"Whole wheat, multi-grain or gluten free?"

I thought, *Christ...did someone in their corporate office sit around all day thinking of ways to make this so damn difficult?* "None of the above," I said curtly. "Do you have any made with real flour?"

"No. Just whole wheat, multi-grain or gluten free."

"Fine. I'll take the whole wheat."

"How do you want it toasted?"

I rolled my eyes and said, "Almost burnt."

"Regular cream cheese or low-fat?"

"You're kidding?" I said, incredulously.

She just stared at me.

I looked at her name tag and asked, "Is your nickname 'Twenty-question Sarah?'" She didn't respond. Instead, she asked again—as if she were an automaton—"Regular cream cheese or low-fat?"

"Regular. I'm not counting anything except the time it's taken me to order a cup of coffee and a toasted bagel."

"And your name for the order, please?" she said, without looking at me.

"Avi." I gave that name out of spite. Amazingly, she didn't have twenty questions about it. *I'm sure she never attended a yeshiva*, I thought. "Do you also need my social security number?"

No response from her other than, "That will be $7.90." She swiped the gift card, and handed it back to me. "You have $22.10 left on the card. You can wait over there for your order. We'll call you when it's ready."

I was afraid to ask, but deemed it necessary: "Could I get the coffee with cream?"

"You'll find the condiments on the other side of the counter from where you pick up your order. There's whole milk, skim milk, organic milk and half and half."

"Of course." And with a sarcastic smile, I said, "Wouldn't have expected anything less."

As I was waiting with the others—including the two women who each ordered a large, white something-or-other with whipped cream—I heard the voice from behind me ask the question.

The Palestinian had an ever-so-slight British accent, and a broad, hefty smile showing off his perfectly white, straight teeth. From his speech and smile, he didn't appear to be someone who grew up in a ghetto in Gaza.

"I'm surprised you know Arabic," he said. "You spoke it flawlessly. I thought you would have responded with the Hebrew greeting, 'Shalom.'"

"The same thought crossed my mind. You knew I was Jewish, but chose to greet me in Arabic. That said, I always respond in kind," I said snarkily.

"Ah, yes...a hint of hostility," he said still smiling. He paused. "My greeting was more natural, as it is my native tongue. No offense meant. Nonetheless, I appreciate your greeting and the effort behind it."

Just then, a young man behind the counter shouted, "Avi. Coffee and bagel." I realized then that I should have ordered more, as I had worked up an appetite just placing it.

I grabbed my nourishment. Before I went searching for a quiet table where there were no electronic devices in use, and doused my coffee with half and half, I turned to the Palestinian. With the same intensity in my voice as in my glare, I said, "Don't confuse hostility with suspicion."

He dropped the smile.

I found that table, and assumed I would be able to savor my feast in peace. I was wrong. The Palestinian stood next to me and asked, "May I join you?" He was also eating light. He had tea and a Danish of some kind. I wondered if they had given him the third degree as well.

I didn't want company, but I also didn't want to appear rude—although that rarely stopped me before. But the kid had a pleasant demeanor, if not intrusive, and was dressed in a preppy manner. It wasn't as if he just stepped off the boat.

I said, with no welcoming smile or tone, "Please. Have a seat...*across* from me where I can see your hands."

"That's quite insulting."

"Then find another seat. I wasn't looking for company."

I sipped my regular coffee and started to spread my non fat-free cream cheese on my barely-toasted bagel. Holding it over my lighter would have toasted it darker.

To my astonishment, and disappointment, the Palestinian appeared directly across from me. He put down his food, sat, and then laid both of his hands on the table—palms up. It seemed to me he had done this before.

"There. Satisfied?" He appeared greatly annoyed. But I wasn't sure if his irritation was directed at me, my request, or his compliance. "Are you checking for weapons, or just want to see if I washed before eating?"

Good comeback I thought, and chuckled to myself. "Both," I said, slightly looking up. "I like to know I'll be able to finish my meal. Old habit from Vietnam. And I have a fetish for cleanliness." He didn't appear to have any weapons, and his hands were clean. "As I said, don't confuse hostility with suspicion."

"But why would you be suspicious? I don't believe I've given you any reason."

This time I did look up, and at him. I gave a one-word answer: "History."

We both sat in refreshing silence for a few moments. I was fixated on my bland bagel. Then, he started up again.

"Is Avi your given name?" he said in a more congenial tone.

I sighed and said, slightly exasperated, "No. It's Allen. Avi is just a carryover from my youth."

"Mine is Abdul-Basir Al Hamdani," and enthusiastically stuck out his hand. "Pleasure to meet you."

Once again I was faced with a decision. *Why can't I just order and eat without being interrogated? I can't remember the last time I had to make so many useless decisions.* I put down my plastic knife and shook his hand, but didn't look directly at him. I couldn't bring myself to say, 'Pleasure to meet you as well.' Instead I offered up, "Abdul-Basir. 'Servant of the All-Seeing.' Correct?"

The young man dropped his Danish. "I am indeed impressed, Avi." Then he caught himself. "My apologies for using that name. That was quite presumptuous of me."

"No harm done, Abdul-Basir. I opened that door," I said, still preparing my bagel for consumption.

A profound look of relief crossed his face. "Then call me Basir, if it pleases you."

"What would please me more…Basir…is if you would allow me to drink my overpriced coffee, and eat this poor resemblance of a bagel before they both get cold. Cold coffee I can handle, but not a cold bagel with cream cheese. Especially *this* bagel."

"Absolutely. But if I may ask just one more question?"

"Is your nickname, 'Twenty-question Basir?'"

He stared at me, not knowing what I was asking.

"Never mind," I said. "It's an inside joke. Go ahead. Ask your question."

"Thank you."

"You're welcome." I said under my breath, "Something tells me you would have asked it no matter what my answer was." He didn't hear me. If he did, he ignored my comment.

He fiddled with his tea for a moment, and then asked, "How did you know the meaning of my name? I mean, I've been studying at Columbia University for almost four years now, and not one person, not one, outside of the other Arabic students who already knew, has ever asked me the meaning of my name."

"I'm a virtual cornucopia of useless knowledge, Basir. And I've also been to Israel many times to visit friends. There are things you learn through osmosis."

"Very interesting, Avi. Are you afraid when you visit Israel?"

I looked squarely at him and snapped back, "No. Should I be?"

"No. But there are…risks."

"From whom? You and your friends?"

He shot back defiantly, "I've never done any act of civil disobedience or terror."

"Never? Really? You've never tossed a rock, a bomb, or a Molotov cocktail at an Israeli patrol or tank? Never launched a rocket into an unsuspecting civilian neighborhood?"

His coal-black eyes burst into flames, and he pounded his right fist on the table: "I said *never*, Avi, and I meant never!" A couple seated near us looked over, greatly miffed we had interrupted their bond with their devices. I paid them no mind. I made no apologies. *Well…that struck a nerve,* I thought. *Let's see where this goes.*

He composed himself, and continued: "My parents would not have tolerated that type of behavior. Some of my former friends have, and still do, but not me."

"So, you do have friends who are engaged in acts of terror?"

"I said former friends. And they are acts of civil disobedience, not terror."

"Yeah. One man's act of civil disobedience is another man's terror. So why are they your *former* friends?"

The level of his voice dropped, as did his head. "They want nothing to do with me. They are ashamed of me." He reflected for a moment, then raised his head and spoke directly at me: "And why do you keep associating me with those who engage in acts of terror? I'm not now, nor have I ever been a terrorist. I've never injured another human."

"Like I said…history."

"You may not believe this, but not all Palestinians embrace the same history."

I wanted to say, 'You're right. I don't believe you.' But I kept my mouth shut—surprisingly. Instead, I pivoted. "Well, there are risks here, Basir. Besides, I stay with friends when I'm in Israel. Most served in the I.D.F. Some served with Mosaad. Are you afraid here?"

"It is true. There have been times when I have been concerned for my safety." His demeanor again became more solemn. "But I am more concerned for my safety when I go back home, which I haven't done in awhile, much to the dismay of my parents and siblings."

"And why is that? That you're concerned for your safety back home?"

Basir again bowed his head, and spoke in a subdued tone: "Because I have not taken up the same cause some of my childhood friends have. They believe I am not among the faithful—that I have betrayed them."

"Have you, betrayed them?" and took another sip of my coffee, and a bite out of my bagel.

"I don't believe so. I believe in the same outcome, just not the manner in which to achieve it. Violence only begets violence."

"There's a time for everything. Violence is one of them."

"Perhaps. But not toward the innocent."

My tone softened. "On that, we both agree." I pressed on: "And you believe these...former friends of yours may try to harm you?"

"I do not know. That is what concerns me."

Let's see how far I can push this. "And what cause, exactly, are we speaking of?" although I knew what cause it was.

I sensed he didn't want to venture any further into this conversation. I really didn't want to either, and quickly pulled back. I spoke with a calm, but yet commanding voice, "Don't answer that."

He gave an involuntary deep sigh of relief that we weren't going to pursue that discussion. We both knew the outcome could have—no, more than likely would have—been explosive. So I changed the subject. "What's with the British accent?"

"You are indeed observant, Avi. My compliments. Both of my parents are doctors and completed their undergraduate studies in England. They sent me there, to a boarding school, when I turned eight years old. I didn't want to go and be so far from home for such a long time, but they insisted it was best for me."

"Yeah. Been there, done that," now fully engaged with my bagel.

"Your parents sent you to a boarding school as well?"

I wanted to explain my religious exile and imprisonment, and to add, 'Does reform school count?' but decided he wouldn't understand, and I was in no mood to explain. "No, not exactly. But I had the same feelings through some of my schooling. And so did my parents." I quickly asked another question. "So how did you wind up at Columbia?"

"My father made that decision for me. He and my mother studied medicine there. That's where they met."

"Where would you have preferred to study?"

"I would have been content at Tel Aviv University. It would have been closer to home and it would have been a first-rate education."

"But Columbia has a more worldwide reputation. Besides, didn't you say you were afraid of going home?"

He became adamant, and said almost shouting, "I said I was *concerned* for my safety. I didn't say I was afraid!" Basir paused, and lowered his voice: "But it's still home," and took a deep breath. "This is not."

I could see tears forming in his eyes.

I knew that feeling—what it felt like to be away from home. In addition to being shipped off to Brooklyn every summer and my stints in reform school, I served seven years in the Navy. Part of that was a combat tour on river boats in Vietnam—where I was wounded, and then recuperated for four months at a military hospital in Hawaii—and the other part was serving onboard a Fast Attack submarine based at Pearl. I had no desire to go home, but I missed it all the same.

"Hey, Basir, I know you won't believe this, but I do understand what you're feeling. I really do." I continued with the questions. It's just my nature. "So, are you going to become a doctor?"

"I'm not sure, but I have to decide very soon. I'm in my senior year."

"I think I know the answer to this question, but I'm going to ask it anyway. What do your parents want you to do?"

"We both know the answer to that question, Avi."

"What do you want to do? After all, it is your life."

At that question, he became more passionate: "I want to pursue mathematics. I'm good at it, and I love it. Many of my professors have encouraged me to follow that path."

"So do it! What's holding you back?"

"The disapproval and disappointment of my parents…and money."

"Yeah. Know that feeling as well. Seems that's universal with kids and parents. Same shit, different culture." I've been on both sides of that equation, having raised three children. Disappointment and disapproval go both ways—even between spouses.

Basir leaned forward, "I believe I know what you mean. I see it every day with the American students, but more so with the foreign ones. If I don't pursue a medical degree, I'm concerned my parents will not help me to finance my extended education."

"Concerned or afraid? Which one?"

"Both, Avi. There is no way I could afford to finance my own advanced degree. It's difficult enough for those who are born here. No one would lend me the money." He started to fidget with his plastic spoon. There was anxiety in his voice when he said, "But if I do become a doctor, my parents will want me to practice in Gaza and in Israel, as they do. They are apolitical and well-respected in both places. But they, too, come under a great deal of pressure from all sides, as I would. I am not as strong as they are. I truly don't know what to do."

This kid is caught between a rock and a hard place. I'd been there many times—unfortunately. But I was stronger than he appeared to be. I had to be. I had no safety net. For most of my life I had to rely on myself. Some of that was by choice. Some of it was…because….well…I brought it on myself.

I attempted another angle for the young Palestinian to consider, although I didn't quite understand why. "You've probably played cricket, correct?"

"Of course. And I'm quite good, if I may say so myself."

"Well, I'm a big baseball fan. And there's a saying: 'swinging for the fences.'"

"We have a different saying, but I know the meaning."

"What do you think it means?"

"You go for it. Try and get the home run and perhaps even win the game."

"But you might strike out or otherwise fail to get it out of the park."

"That's true, Avi. But one never knows until one tries."

As he said that, I saw an *aha!* look on his face. He just sat there, staring into space, as if he were watching a movie playing inside his head. Then he nodded his head in agreement. It appeared Basir had come to some conclusion. *Perhaps he finally made the connection, and now believes he can change his own future. Perhaps he came to the conclusion that he is stronger than he thought.*

And then something strange happened to me; something I never thought would happen between me and a Palestinian. *Am I feeling empathy for Basir?* We shared some similar experiences, and both of us had had decisions to make. Maybe neither of us realized at the time that they came with consequences—some of them negative. I know I didn't. But we made them nonetheless.

I had swung for the fences many times and was willing to let the chips fall where they may. Basir had already done it once before—even if he hadn't realized he had—and I believed he was ready to do it again. Perhaps he was more prepared this time.

Funny thing happens, though, when you swing for the fences: whether you get a home run or strike out, there will always be those who will say you made the wrong decision. It's bad enough we second guess ourselves; but even when we don't, there will always be those who will. Fuck 'em.

"What's on your mind, Basir?"

"I think…no, I believe I have a solution to my dilemma."

"And what is it?"

"Forgive me, Avi, but I would rather not say at this time. I'm not quite confident of all the details or ramifications. But it is a solution, or at least a plan."

I gave up a genuine smile, and said, "Good for you. A plan is better than nothing. But do you know what validates a plan?"

"Please tell me."

"Acting on it."

Basir looked relieved—more relieved than he had during the entire conversation. There was an assurance about him. I was confident that, whatever his plan was, he would somehow, someway, make it work—and I was happy for him.

At that moment, several thoughts raced through me. *What the hell just happened? And what was happening to me? Was I going soft? At any other time, I would have told this kid to buzz off. That it was his problem to solve, not mine. I would have said good luck—maybe—but certainly would have said goodbye.*

I was as finished with my coffee and bagel as I would ever be. "I should be going, Basir, as I have some errands to run. But before I go, I have just one more question."

"Certainly, Avi. What is it?"

"What brings you here, to my city?"

"My roommate is from your city. He lives close by, and generously invited me to stay with his family over our winter break. Interestingly enough, he is Jewish. And…his father is a doctor!"

Who would have thought? "That doesn't surprise me. This is a very affluent neighborhood, mostly made up of professionals, and there are many Jewish families who reside here."

"Do you reside here?"

"Nope. I live on the other side of town. It's not quite as affluent, but it's nice, and I call it home. Have you discussed your dilemma with your roommate, or his father?"

"Only with my roommate. He's facing a similar dilemma, and I didn't want to...what's the saying?...'muddy the waters.' He doesn't know how to approach his parents either."

"Yeah. That's the saying. And you were wise not to get in the middle of that situation. *My* compliments on your judgment. Perhaps after you're sure of your plan, you might want to suggest it to him. Then, let him do with it as he sees fit."

"As you did with me!" he said with a new-found resilience. "So, let him decide whether or not to swing for the fences. Is that what you're suggesting?"

"Precisely."

We stood, disposed of our trash—which included half of my bagel, and an unfinished cup of coffee—and ventured onto the parking lot. Before I headed for my car I asked, for some unknown reason, "Do you want a ride?"

"I appreciate the offer, Avi, but I believe I'll walk. It's only a few blocks and I know the way. Besides, it's a nice day and the walk will help me to think through all of this. Perhaps I'll take the long way as it will give me more time."

"Fair enough. Well then, I suppose this is goodbye."

Basir just stood there. Neither of us paid any attention to the cars or people moving about on the lot. Then he said, "Perhaps...if you would agree, of course...we could, you know..."

"Just spit it out!" although I had an idea of what he was going to ask.

"Well, keep in touch. Communicate from time to time. I know I would enjoy hearing from you, Avi. I don't have many people...actually...I have no one, to really confide in. And I found it very easy to converse with you."

"Really? Not many have ever said that. And I certainly didn't expect you to hold that sentiment. I wasn't exactly welcoming to you at first. But to answer your question, yes, I would enjoy hearing from you as well." I was stunned. The words just fell out of my mouth.

He lit up that broad smile, and said, "Don't confuse hostility with suspicion—right, Avi?" and gave a deep belly laugh. I smiled and laughed as well. *This kid has some moxie.*

I reached for my pen, but realized I had nothing to write on. I said, "Don't move, Basir. I'll be right back."

I went inside and grabbed a napkin. I didn't want to ask any of the staff if they had some scrap paper. And thank God I had a pen. I could only imagine the myriad of questions that would have been hurled my way: 'Do you want a pen or pencil? Black or blue ink? Gel or regular ink? How big of a piece of paper? Recycled or new?' My head was swimming.

I wrote my e-mail address and cell phone number on it, and brought it back to Basir, who was patiently waiting. "Here. You'll find all of my contact info on the napkin. I'll get your e-mail address when you write to me."

"So you're counting on me to write first?"

"You got it, Basir. It's on you."

"Fair enough, Avi."

"Just do me one favor."

"And what might that be?"

"Don't share this with any of your *former* friends back home. I don't need to be on any government watch list," and feigned a scowl.

Basir looked mortified, until he saw me crack a smile. He laughed and said, "Ah, you're just fooling with me, Avi…" and then the same concerned look crossed his face, "aren't you?"

"Yes. I'm just playing."

He gave a sigh of relief and said, "I don't know you well enough to know when you're kidding."

"Remember that. Keep your own counsel. Only share your deepest thoughts and feelings with those whom you believe you can absolutely trust. Unfortunately, you'll find that there will be few of them. I've learned the hard way that you just never know who will attempt to use them against you some day."

"Understand. I have so much to learn."

"For what it's worth, we all have a lot to learn. It never stops…or at least it shouldn't. You're doing fine." His face radiated pride at that comment. He apparently didn't receive too many compliments.

Basir studied the napkin for a few moments, then looked at me and said in his most sincere tone, "You are a wise and generous man, Avi. I believe I can trust you."

I didn't know how to respond—which is usually not the case. I looked down, nodded my head, then looked directly at him and said, "Again, not sentiments most people hold about me, but thank you. You're a thoughtful young man. And I believe I can trust you as well."

Again he smiled. Then a melancholy look came over him. "Well then, I should be on my way, Avi, as you must. Perhaps we can meet here again."

"Not here. I don't like this place."

He became animated. "I know what you mean, Avi. The tea is putrid and overpriced; the Danish selection is limited and not always fresh; they're always crowded; and everyone is on their laptop or tablet. They've lost the art of spirited conversation, which is another reason I enjoyed my time with you. You were not afraid to speak your mind in a civil manner."

I had to laugh at his assessment of Starbucks, and that he believed

I spoke my mind in a civil manner. Yet another attribute most would not assign to me. But he was spot on about the attachment people have to their machines. Whatever happened to two people just sharing coffee and conversation?

He continued, "Perhaps we could meet at one of your local diners. I have been to a few in New York and New Jersey, and I know of one not too far from here. My roommate has taken me there on several occasions. They are much more welcoming, far less intrusive, and inexpensive. After all, I am still a student on a limited stipend. I have also become quite fond of the American breakfast…minus the bacon, of course."

"Of course. That would work for me, Basir. You and I share the same taste in food and venue. I know several places, and the one you speak of. Drop me a line, or call. I'm sure we can work out a time. How long will you be in town?"

"For about another week." He then said with childish enthusiasm, "I promise I'll write, or call, or both. And one more thing, Avi."

"What's that?"

"Please call me, perhaps in about a year or so, should you have the opportunity to visit Israel."

"And why is that?"

"Because that is part of my plan—to be back home."

"Outstanding! I sincerely hope you make it work. Also make it part of your plan to talk with your parents. You might find them to be more supportive than you think. And I promise to see you if, and when, I return to Israel." I paused. "Then it's settled. Breakfast, and possibly a visit with you in Israel. I look forward to both."

"I know you must be on your way, Avi." He stuck out his hand. This time I didn't hesitate to shake it, or say, "It was a pleasure meeting you, Abdul-Basir."

"So you see, Avraham, two people can change history…yes?"

"Yeah. That's usually the way it happens. One person at a time."

Basir remembered how he greeted me at first, and switched it up. "Shalom, my friend."

I responded in kind. I always do. "Shalom. Peace be with you, my *friend*."

We separated, but something told me our lives would forever be attached.

What the hell just happened?

4

Benjamin Stahlman, Scholar

Eight years ago I decided to get a college degree—after a dozen years with my employer. My career seemed stalled, advancement-wise and financially. To upper management's way of thinking, experience is secondary to a degree. My marriage was already on the down slope. If I couldn't salvage the marriage, at least I had a chance to save my career.

My decision was met with a healthy dose of skepticism from my parents—although they were certainly supportive—and a great deal of derision from the ex. With her, it's always been about one-upmanship and, of course, money. She already had a degree and a good job. Perhaps she was jealous that I would end up with the same level of education. Or perhaps it now would be one less talking point to throw in my face, or to convince our daughter, that I would never amount to much. Candace never missed an opportunity to make that point.

I would counter with, "You always underestimate me."

She would retort, "I don't underestimate you, Ben. In fact, I have never underestimated your propensity for failure."

With that encouragement, I enrolled in night classes at a local private college. I knew it would be a strain working fulltime, attending school at night, and possibly going through a divorce. But I believed the sacrifice of time and financial resources would be worth it. Quite surprisingly, the company was willing to help me to some extent financially, along with scheduling considerations, in return for several additional years of servitude. The balance of funding was derived from loans and grants. For a brief time, dwelling on the amount of money I would eventually owe, I had second thoughts. But after some reflection—which included finishing a bottle of Pinot Grigio—I jumped in.

I wasn't the oldest in my classes; most were in their late forties, or early fifties, attempting to accomplish what I had set out to do. The younger students had come to the realization that they needed real jobs to pay for the mounting debt. We were all making sacrifices. I was not alone.

Although I was cordial, I kept my distance throughout the almost five years it took me to complete my bachelor's degree. Other than the occasional conversation before, or after, classes, I never quite felt like I fit in. I was an in-betweener—not young enough to converse with those in their twenties, and not old enough to have much in common with those in their late forties or fifties.

It was somewhere in my third year that Candace started the divorce proceedings. Thankfully, the ex decided not to drag it out, and about six months later it was done. We thought about selling the house, but knew we would take a financial shellacking. So I agreed to keep the house and pay the mortgage, in lieu of child support—at least that's how it was supposed to be. I still get calls from Candace to pony up money for Andrea's class trips, a new cell phone, and whatever a teenager believes they need. I always respond that we have an agreement, and that I am paying far more than she would have otherwise received in child support. Candace reminds me that I have obligations as a father—not that I've ever forgotten them—and how she still has to pay for some expenses of the now-defunct marital residence when I am short of money—which, admittedly, happens frequently.

One of the proudest moments in my life came the day I finally received my degree. My parents, Andrea, and a few close friends were in attendance. The ex was absent. I suppose it was just too much for Candace to actually see me moving ahead. I had photos taken of me in my cap and gown, degree in hand. Those pictures still hang in my office. Andrea keeps the one with just the two of us on her nightstand.

So there I was: thirty-five, degree in hand, and feeling like I had conquered the world. I had no doubt that I could now finally rise to any level I wanted in the company. No longer would anyone be able to tell me I didn't have the requisite credentials. No one, that is, except my new boss. To him, earning a degree through night school didn't hold the same value as one obtained through "the more traditional route."

"Let's face it, Stahlman, Julian College isn't Harvard. Or even Kansas State. Besides," he would yammer on, "you only have a B.A. Not much use in a business environment. Get a degree in something relevant to business, and then we can talk about advancement."

I always thought, or at least convinced myself, that a degree was a degree. I never had an inclination toward business—even though I had been hustling timeshares for this company since I graduated from high school. Perhaps that's why I chose a liberal arts path, as it gave me exposure to other fields of endeavor. Or perhaps I saw a liberal arts degree as the easiest path. Either way, I had school loans coming due and no more chance to advance financially than when I started on this path.

Not knowing where to turn, I sought out the advice of my philosophy professor, Doctor Priscilla Enfield. She was a stately looking woman—with matching demeanor—in her late fifties or very early sixties, accomplished and well-respected in her field. Hers was the only class where I actually enjoyed doing extra-credit work, or stayed after class to discuss a subject matter in depth. Not many other students, if any, did so. They took the class because it was a requirement. So did I, until I found that it became my Holy Grail. I figured if anyone would be able to give deep and sound advice, it would be her.

The deep part came first: "One does not go into philosophical studies to make a great living, but does so for the love, passion, and pursuit of truth. Furthermore, in order to teach it, which is probably one of the few ways you will ever make any kind of a living pursuing this path, you'll need to obtain your doctorate, or at very least a master's degree. However, Benjamin, that is not your dilemma, is it?" She always had a keen sense of the obvious.

"No, it's not, Professor," as if she needed confirmation—which she didn't. "My real dilemma is what to do with what appears to be a useless degree, and a mountain of debt now coming due."

What followed was the sound part of her advice: "Stay in school. As long as you are in school, you can defer your loans."

"I didn't know that, Dr. Enfield. But then I just dig myself deeper in debt."

"That is true, but at least with a master's you can advance in your own company, or perhaps move on to other companies that value advanced degrees, even if it wasn't obtained *'through the more traditional route.'*"

"And what studies do you believe I should pursue?"

"Well, you seem to have the temperament, aptitude, and attitude required for the study of philosophy. And you do enjoy it, do you not?"

"I do, but..."

"But what, Benjamin?"

"Other than teaching, for which I really don't have the temperament or the inclination, how will acquiring an advanced degree in philosophy advance my career?"

"Many businesses now have those on their staff who have an understanding and appreciation for ethics, and philosophy lends itself to that discipline. After all, one may know what is ethical, and what is not, but not why it is so. Philosophy helps us to understand the *why*."

"Yeah. I'm not sure if now is the time." *I'm not sure if any time would be the right time,* I thought. *I'm tired of going to school and getting nowhere. But, I need some relief from all of this debt. My choices are limited. No...they're pretty damn much nonexistent.*

"Trust me on this, Benjamin. There will never be a better time in your life to pursue this endeavor than now, for many reasons. Think about it. If you wish to discuss it further, you know where to find me. Here's my cell number if you wish to talk further."

I thanked her and headed home to digest what I had just heard, along with another bottle of wine. I have always found that wine makes me less inhibited so I'm able to think more freely—at least that's what I've convinced myself. Even when it doesn't, I still feel better during the consumption of said beverage, although I usually don't feel that way the next day. I suppose there are always trade-offs.

I took the professor's advice and found a master's program that would accept me. It was about an hour away, and would require the company to adjust my work schedule to accommodate classes and travel time. I also learned, much to my dismay, the considerable expense it would entail.

As unpleasant a task as it was, the next step was to pitch my boss—Peter Herrington, the V.P. of Sales—on how my getting a master's in philosophy would help them navigate the tricky waters of business ethics. "You may have stumbled onto something, Stahlman," he said in his usual condescending tone. "This industry is constantly being scrutinized for its selling tactics. I believe we do everything above board, but I suppose perception is reality. Is this going to be another one of your night school degrees?"

I responded tentatively, "Yes, Mr. Herrington."

"Where do you intend to get this degree?"

"Southeastern University. It's about an hour from here."

"I know that school. It has a decent reputation. My daughter was accepted there, but decided to go somewhere more prestigious. I'm surprised you were accepted. But I suppose your money is as good as the next person's."

He paused. Then he said, "Well, even though it won't be obtained through the more traditional route, I suppose it can't hurt. Besides, no one outside of this company has to know. They probably wouldn't care. Perception is reality. Right, Stahlman?"

"Correct."

"Then let's just keep that between the two of us. No sense making that distinction public. Agreed?"

"Agreed, Mr. Herrington."

I sat there, holding my breath as he walked around his corner office contemplating our discussion. After several excruciating minutes, Herrington pulled up a chair next to me and said, "Okay, Stahlman. We'll front some of the expenses and make the schedule adjustments. But you'd better keep up your sales and get at least a B average. And, of course, I expect you to stick around for at least three years after you've obtained your degree. We do need to recoup our investment."

"Of course, Mr. Herrington."

"Excellent. I'll prepare the document on our agreement. Just give me a written proposal as to the finances you'll need. I'll take care of the rest. And, Stahlman?"

"Yes, Mr. Herrington?"

"This better be worth it, and you'd better live up to your end of the agreement. We're clear on this?"

"Absolutely!"

"Outstanding." He stood and walked toward the door. I followed. "I expect that proposal on my desk in two days. Now…you have sales to make, and I have a luncheon to attend," and he walked out of his office. *Son of a bitch didn't even shake my hand.*

I rolled the dice and aimed high on my funding proposal. What did I have to lose? Maybe, just maybe, the company would front the whole nut. But if they didn't, I knew I could make up the difference from additional loans and grants.

With acceptance from the college and about two-thirds of the funding in hand, I enrolled and was now granted a reprieve from paying my existing school loans. I am not a religious person, but I did my share of praying that I was making the correct decision. This time, however, I did not seek out the advice of friends and family, as I had made up my mind and wanted no counter arguments. I didn't want to confuse the issue with whatever truth they had to offer, which was somewhat of a paradox for someone wanting to pursue enlightenment.

Nonetheless, once family and friends learned about it, I did get my share of post-mortem opinions—like a coroner rendering a decision after the autopsy. While some were supportive, most—mainly

Candace—shared their doubts as to the usefulness of advanced studies in philosophy. In the end, I paid them no mind.

The beginning of my master's program was an eye-opener, especially my two classes in the first semester. Both classes were taught by philosophy Ph.D.s, who were no-nonsense guys. They didn't see themselves as babysitters. As far as they were concerned, they were paid to impart their vast knowledge and you paid to receive it. They would not stand for your wasting their time.

One class was populated by grad students who were taking philosophy as a general requirement. Again, I was the outsider—the old man. However, I had some stature as I had already been through a philosophy course as an undergrad, and I actually had life experience. I was, as it turned out, the smartest guy in the room—next to the professor, of course. I felt like a giant among midgets.

The other class was a different proposition; keeping my distance was not an option. Smaller, it was dominated by students who were philosophy majors. Although all were about the same age as those in the other class, these students had studied and were conversant with the writings of the great philosophers—past and present. Now, for the first time in my college career, I truly felt intimidated. I was not the old man with life experience. I most definitely was not the smartest guy in the room.

For the first half of the semester, I was—as far as the other students were concerned, and I'm pretty sure as far as the professor was concerned, as well—dead weight. No matter how much I studied, I stumbled through answers, and felt all eyes burn into me each and every time I was called upon. I could see them—students and professor, alike—shake their heads, smirking with looks of disparagement. So I reset my study schedule, putting in twice as many hours.

By the second half of that semester I started to come into my own. Heads nodded in approval at my answers. Where the professor would eviscerate some of the students during certain exercises, he would politely correct my answers. I don't believe he did that because he necessarily liked me more than them, I believe he did so because he saw I was actually starting to get it. I received an A in both of those classes—one of the few who did. Gone were the smirks; gone were the condescending looks.

The remaining three years it took me to finish my degree went well. I managed to hold the requisite B average and received my big reward—a Master of Arts in philosophy—to the delight of my daughter, my parents, and Dr. Enfield.

Absent, again, was my ex. Not absent, however, were the calls from her asking me how I was going to pay back the monumental debt I had accumulated. I told her that it was none of her business. I'm pretty sure that her concern was not for my financial well-being, as I detected a not-so-subtle hint of envy. There was even a smidgeon of anger in her voice. It seems Andrea had asked her mother, "When are you going to get your master's degree?" Touché.

My promotion came through and I received a decent increase in pay. We now have a Business Ethics department—albeit a department of one. And guess who's the manager? However, it was still not enough to pay back the loans and maintain my current lifestyle, which included paying for all of Andrea's new necessities—like the umpteenth pair of Abercrombie or American Eagle jeans, or fresh Nike sneakers.

I started to question what I had done. And once again, I sought out the advice of my mentor.

"So, I now have my master's, Dr. Enfield, and a better position at the company. But I still don't feel satisfied. Why is that?"

Dr. Enfield looked at me incredulously for a few moments. It appeared as if she wanted to laugh, but restrained herself. Then, she finally responded, "You're the one with the master's in philosophy, Benjamin. Suppose you tell me?"

I knew it had nothing to do with being satisfied, but everything to do with how in hell I was going to repay these loans, and she knew it. "It's the loans, Dr. Enfield. I'm worried how I will repay them, and that's the truth."

I caught her rolling her eyes. Then she asked, "What did we discuss a little over three years ago?"

"That as long as I am in school, the loans are deferred. But I can't do that indefinitely, can I? Sooner or later they will come due. I mean, how much more schooling can I do?"

"As much as you want to, Benjamin, or at least until you find a position that pays well enough to cover the loans."

Finding a new position was off the table, as I still had my contractual servitude. But the loans were coming due. "Is that what you did?"

"Does it really matter what I did?" I couldn't quite determine if she was annoyed, or patronizing me. She continued, "This is your life we're talking about, Benjamin, not mine. I made my decision long ago. Now it's time to make yours." *Yeah. Definitely annoyed.*

"Any suggestions, Professor?"

Her tone became more accommodating. "There is always a doctorate. I'll even help you with the process."

"And how long will it take for me to get a doctorate?"

"Perhaps another three to five years."

My eyes grew wide. I gulped and all but shouted, "Three to five years?" *That almost sounded like a prison sentence.* "Hell, at the outside of that time frame, Doctor Enfield, I'll be…forty-three!"

She politely grinned. "Not exactly an old man, Benjamin. Besides, how old will you be in five years if you don't obtain a doctorate?"

I answered sheepishly, "Forty-three."

"There you go." She smiled. "Whether or not you pursue your studies, you'll still be the same age, except without the opportunities an advanced degree can offer."

"Then there's the additional debt, Professor."

"Trust me on this, Benjamin. There will never be a better time in your life to pursue this endeavor than now, for many reasons. Think about it. Do you want my assistance or not?"

"I'll get back to you soon, Dr. Enfield. I need some time to weigh my options."

What I really needed to weigh was another bottle of wine. After finishing it off that night, I had my answer. I rather liked the sound of Doctor Stahlman.

In vino veritas.

5

Wooden Statements

The trip to Charleston, South Carolina would take thirteen hours. Eleven hours in, I pulled into a rest stop to stretch my legs. One last respite before the final push.

The grounds were a throwback to a more innocent time—when travel was an adventure, not an objective. It was a departure from the sterile sites along other interstates. I found a quiet spot, bordered by wooden rails, to savor my soda—retrieved from the sole vending machine—and smoke a cigarette. Near me was a young man practicing Tai Chi, in slow motion, among the trees. As I watched, the sounds of the highway faded. It was then I noticed weathered carvings on the rails. They seemed to fall into categories.

Love found: "Brandon and Chrissie 4ever." Love lost: "Drop dead Jesse. Go to Hell. Good riddance." Comings: "Finally home." Goings: "I hate this state. Can't wait to leave." And apathy: "Who cares? You're all losers." All of them micro vignettes—the original social media.

The etchings had no dates. I wondered if Brandon and Chrissie were still together and blissfully in love. What did Jesse do to piss off whomever? Who was coming home? From where? How long had they been away? What happened to cause anonymous to hate an entire state? And where were they going in such a hurry?

"Who cares?" Someone cared enough to read and comment; carving is slow work. Perhaps that person had some—or all—of the same experiences and no longer felt the need to explain. Or maybe just gave up on life. And why the insult? Was it self-incrimination?

The road was waiting. I still had my own journey to complete, but I wanted answers. So I carved my proclamation: "Tell me more."

6

The Box

"A box is selfless," said John, my co-worker and friend. It was his concluding declaration to our conversation, before we started to repack our trophies into the boxes from which they came.

John and I were invited to the annual awards banquet, as we were among the top sales associates in the company. Although both of us joined the company at about the same time, this was the first awards ceremony for me, and the second for John. He received *Rookie of the Year* honors the previous year. John wasn't able to attend that ceremony, and neither of us really wanted to be at this one. Neither of us is comfortable with that much attention. But when the V.P. of the department "Requests your presence…", it's job-security suicide not to attend. So, there we were.

"Just look at this box, Allen, it's a work of art," is how John started the conversation. He gazed at the box in wonderment, as a child would after opening a birthday or Christmas gift. "I mean, it's so…symmetrical."

Anyone familiar with us knew exactly what he meant. There was nothing on our desks, or standing partition walls, that would give anyone insight into our personal lives. On our desks were a computer and phone. The only items displayed on our walls were company policies or job-related information—and they were framed and hung in perfect balance and symmetry. One would have thought we had measured the distance up from the desks, and between each frame, with a laser. We didn't; we just used a ruler, although the thought of using a laser did cross our minds.

"The box is sturdy and the lid fits so tightly that when you replace it the air rushes out onto your fingertips. Feel it?" he asked, as he demonstrated several times. I tried it with my box and found he was correct.

"Even the fabric covering the box is perfectly fitted both inside and out. What craftsmanship. Whoever made the box obviously knew what they were doing, more so than the person who designed and built this Lucite piece of crap," he said holding up the trophy. "To me, a box is sometimes more important than the thing inside of it."

He waxed on philosophically for several more minutes, extolling the virtues of a box. "It holds, preserves, and protects memories—those things we cherish and perhaps want to pass down to future generations." He then added in a hushed voice, "It can hold secrets."

"It's also used to bury people," I said in a somber tone, remembering family and friends I loved, and lost. "But…I suppose that goes along with most of what you just said." John made no comment; he just nodded his head in agreement.

After a few moments John broke the silence. "So, Allen, what are you going to put in yours?"

"My military medals and the flag I received from my father's funeral. How about you?

"Not sure yet, but I know it won't be this stupid trophy. The box is too good for that. In fact, I believe it would be an insult to the box," he said and laughed, doing his best to lighten the mood.

One of the other recipients, who knew us well, caught the tail end of the conversation and joined in—uninvited, of course. "So…are you guys going to put the awards on your desks?" he inquired with a devilish smile.

"Nooooo," John and I said in unison, with a dismissive tone and look.

"Symmetry. It would break the symmetry," I said, "as there would be nothing on the other side of the desk to balance it out."

"Besides," said John, "it would just be one more thing we would have to dust, which is why I'm not even going to display it at home." I made no comment and just shrugged my shoulders.

"So, don't you want others to see what you've accomplished?" asked the uninvited quest.

"Not necessary," I responded crisply. "You know what we accomplished. The rest of the company knows what we accomplished. More importantly, John and I know what we've accomplished. As far as I'm concerned, we're the only ones who count." Actually, I wasn't entirely sure I believed all of what I was saying. John's smile said all of what he was thinking.

"What…ever," said the other recipient, shaking his head. "I don't know about you guys, but I'm going to take advantage of the open bar." Then he offered up one last dig. "It's just a stupid box. You guys know that…right?" He turned and walked away, without waiting for an answer.

"Asshole," John commented, stating the obvious. "He just doesn't get it."

That's when John offered his "selfless" comment. We both smiled and finished the repacking.

Although neither of us are big drinkers, we agreed to partake of the company's generosity at the open bar. On our way over, though, I started to seriously question my decision about not displaying the trophy on my office desk. After all, I did earn it.

If I displayed it, John might think I betrayed him.

If I didn't, the company might think I didn't appreciate their award. I felt slightly embarrassed that—at my age—I might be caving to peer pressure. Was I?

A few days after the ceremony I came to a decision. It was one that I was not entirely pleased with, and pretty sure no one else would be either. I would display the trophy on one side of the desk, balance it out with the box on the other side, and dust both with the Swiffer I kept in my desk drawer.

There. Problem solved. No one's happy. Hopefully, next year, they just give us gift cards.

7

Separated at Birth

All parties were present in the attorney's conference room. Gertrude Heller and her oldest son, Henry, had traveled from Florida and sat next to each other on one side of the spacious table; Ian Heller, her youngest son, sat on the other. They were contentious, opposing parties in every sense of the word. The attorney—a family friend and Gertrude's long-time counsel—sat at the head. This was uncomfortable for Gertrude, the matter-at-hand aside. She was used to always being seated at the head of any table since her husband passed away thirty years earlier. The attorney was not only there to officiate and give legal advice for these proceedings, but also to act as referee.

Every year Gertrude Heller made four pilgrimages from Pennsylvania to Florida—one trip per season—to stay with Henry. Normally her stays would last no more than a month at most, and then she would return home to gloat to her friends about how wonderful it was to be with him. She almost never mentioned how good it was to be home with Ian.

Henry would always send Ian an e-mail with their mother's flight itinerary. It was Ian's task to print it out and give it to her. But this last time there was a noticeable difference. Ian didn't ask his mother about it; he knew if he did she just would have said, "Ask your brother. Henry makes all the arrangements. He always does." Although Ian found talking to his brother almost as distasteful as talking to his mother, the question nonetheless begged to be asked. Ian decided Henry was the lesser of two evils.

"Hey kid, what's up?" Henry always answered a call from Ian the same way. Even though Ian was now in his mid-sixties, Henry called Ian "kid" just to make the point—like an alpha dog—that he was five years older. Henry took the role of being the big brother with the same solemnity and seriousness as if he were a Knight Templar guarding the Holy Grail.

"Not much, Henry." This was Ian's usual response, as he never wanted to give Henry any opening to ask questions about his life. Ian knew that whatever he told his brother would find its way back to their mother as soon as he and Henry hung up. Ian guarded his life, and his privacy, with the same passion as the Spartans defended the Hot Gates at Thermopylae.

Henry knew this would be Ian's go-to answer. "So, why the call?"

"I got the itinerary and printed it out, but noticed there was no return flight. Did I miss something?"

"No, Mom didn't want a return flight. She said she would decide that when she got here."

"Whose idea was that?" Ian never missed an opportunity to poke a finger in Henry's proverbial eye.

"What's that supposed to mean?"

"It means whose idea was it for her not to want a return ticket, that's all." But Henry knew what Ian meant.

Henry did not even attempt to hide his irritation at being challenged. "It was her idea. I did as Mom instructed, Ian."

Yeah...you're her bitch. You always do as Mom instructs, Ian said to himself. "Well...it's her visit. I suppose she can stay as long as she likes," he said, with a not-so-subtle hint of glee. Before Henry could launch into one of his usual sermons about how Ian should be a more loving and doting son—like he was—Ian cut off the conversation: "Gotta go, Henry. I'll give Mom the itinerary"—and he hung up.

The animus between Ian and his mother and brother started long before that call and that flight itinerary, and before Ian found himself forfeiting much of his life these past seven years to care for his now ninety-three-year-old mother almost daily, since he and his mother happened to live in the same city. Henry always professed a greater affection for, and devotion to, his mother. Yet he made sure he kept at least five states between him and her for over forty years. Even when she was hospitalized on several occasions for minor falls or some other ailment, Henry's usual excuse—which their mother readily accepted without hesitation or reservation—was that his singing group's schedule didn't allow for side trips to visit her.

But if Ian could not take Gertrude where she wanted or needed to go—and usually without any advance notice (which he needed due to his work schedule)—all hell would break loose, and she would call Henry to complain. Predictably, within minutes, Ian's cell phone would light up. Even though Ian knew he would get a call, he nonetheless would cringe. And just as predictably, Ian would let the call go to voicemail. The resulting message was always deleted without being listened to. When asked by a co-worker why he never listened to the messages, Ian responded, "Why bother? They're just variations on the same theme," and shook his head, sighing in exasperation.

The pattern that followed was always the same—meaning a text or two, or maybe even an e-mail from Henry—asking if Ian got the call and listened to the message. The same thought would always cross Ian's mind: *Christ...doesn't he have anything better to do? He's like a dog with a bone.* "My brother is a freakin' cyber terrorist," Ian commented to the same co-worker. He would finally text back that he had listened to it and that his work schedule didn't allow for spur-of-the-moment changes to chauffeur his mother. No, that animosity started at birth, just as Jacob's and Esau's did.

Henry was conceived on his parent's honeymoon in 1943, just before his father shipped out to England to prepare for D-Day. Gertrude moved to Chicago to be closer to her husband's family, being she didn't have much of one back East. Henry was born in May, 1944, exactly one month before his father hit Omaha beach in Normandy. For over a month, Gertrude Heller didn't know if her husband had survived the invasion, and if her new status would be a widow. Larry Heller, however, made it all the way to the German border, where he received his third and most serious wound in 1945. This one sent him stateside to recover in an Army hospital in Kentucky. He would remain there until the spring of 1946. When Larry finally returned home to Chicago, he was a stranger to Henry. He and Henry never did bond.

Larry eventually agreed to move back East so Gertrude could be in closer proximity to her older sister and estranged father. Ian was born a year later. It was then that Gertrude told her husband, "I raised Henry—he's mine. This one is yours." And that is how Gertrude would henceforth refer to Ian whenever he was in her presence and where there was any conversation or discussion in which Henry's name was uttered in the same sentence: "Henry is…, and This One…" she'd say, pointing to Ian.

Five years is a huge age difference, especially when brothers are being raised and influenced by different parents. They were never kindred spirits, best friends, or playmates. The only thing the brothers shared was a bedroom, and that was by decree when Ian's room was confiscated by eminent domain so it could be converted into a walk-in closet for his mother. The only remnant of Ian's former room was the glass shade covering the ceiling light fixture, depicting four cowboys riding bucking horses. His father installed it when he originally made it into Ian's room. Although Gertrude protested, Larry refused to remove it.

To the most casual observer, it was unclear if the two boys were even brothers. They didn't look alike, with Henry resembling their mother and Ian resembling their father. It was only when all four were together that the puzzle fit, and where it became crystal clear to whom the brothers owed their allegiance. But looks and age weren't the only thing that separated them.

Henry had their mother's temperament: he was argumentative, prone to drama, controlling and demanding, and always had to have the last word. Mother and son shared one view of the world: theirs. They would verbally bludgeon their victims about the head and shoulders with their argument until the intended target surrendered to their point of view. Once either of them got an idea stuck in their heads, it took a stick of dynamite to break it free.

Henry rarely disobeyed his parents, diligently studied, and held part-time jobs from which he dutifully, and willingly, gave his mother her cut. He was a talented musician and singer and that is the path he followed through college, plus a stint with the Navy Band. It eventually became his chosen profession with some rightfully-earned success. When he spoke or wrote of his mother, it was always with admiration and adoration. Gertrude bestowed upon Henry the moniker of the good son.

Ian could not have been more different. He, like his father, had a quiet intellect, was quick-witted with a sharp tongue, and was a voracious reader. Father and son also shared a deep independent and rebellious streak. His father's manifested itself growing up on the streets of the south side of Chicago with his three brothers; Ian gained notoriety with the local police as a juvenile delinquent. And although Ian was a recalcitrant truant, he still had better grades than Henry, much to the chagrin of both Henry and their mother, but to the delight of Ian and their father. Larry Heller always stood between Ian and his mother, no matter what trouble he was in. The same clock made them tick.

Ian also had a hunger for making money, a trait which did not go unnoticed by his maternal grandfather, a bookie. So the boy was running numbers by the time he was ten; by age sixteen, Ian and his best friend became his grandfather's collection agency. He learned from both father and grandfather to keep his own counsel. Ian never told his mother how or what he earned, let alone gave her a cut.

Ian also joined the Navy. But unlike Henry, he didn't stand behind his voice or a musical instrument; he stood behind twin fifty-caliber machine guns on a river boat in Vietnam. Severely wounded when his boat was ambushed, he spent four months recuperating in Hawaii, and then returned to active duty, serving five more years aboard Fast Attack submarines.

It might have seemed to an outsider that Henry and Ian were competing with each other, but no one knew what the prize was. When Ian would speak of his parents, he would only mention his father. If asked about his mother, his response was always, "What about her?"

Gertrude decided Ian was not the good son.

The text message from Henry to Ian was simple enough: "Mom has decided to permanently stay with me in Florida. We need to talk about finances." To Ian, the message might just as well have read: Mom and I need to find a new way to pick your pockets.

"Hey kid, what's up?"

"You text me that Mom is staying in Florida and you wanted to discuss finances—whatever that means. By the way, where is she going to live?"

Henry was rankled that his status of the good son was being called into question, and might possibly be tarnished. "With me, of course. Where did you think she would live?"

Christ...he is so thin-skinned. "In a nursing home. I mean, who's going to take care of her with your travel schedule?"

"I've taken care of that, but you need to share in the expenses. After all, she is our mother."

Whenever Henry would correspond with Ian about how he should be more dutiful, kind, and attentive to their mother—which was at least weekly—he would always write, "After all, she is OUR mother." Somehow, Henry thought putting *our* in caps would strike a more benevolent chord in Ian.

"That's not happening, Henry. I didn't see you come across with any money to help Mom with her expenses when she was living here, or offer to cover any of my expenses for running her around. In fact, I never asked you for a cent. So where do you come off asking me to help front your expenses?"

"Apples and oranges, Ian. She was living in her own house and had the money to pay for her own expenses."

"She still has the money. Use it."

"But who's going to cover her household expenses?"

"Do you know how stupid you sound, Henry? Use her money to pay for her household expenses here and whatever she needs down there, and use your money to care for her. I did. There…is…no…difference. And speaking of caring for her, you were MIA when I was basically living at her house for the month of October while she was recuperating from her fall."

"I was traveling and both you and Mom knew that. I called her every day."

Ian rolled his eyes. "Wow…a phone call. That really helped me. Your travel schedule is always your fallback answer, Henry." The anger in Ian's voice was now tinged with pain. "And where were you and Mom when I was in Hawaii for four months recuperating from my wounds?"

"My God, Ian, that was, what…some forty-five years ago? I can't believe you're still bringing that up. But since you asked, you know they didn't have the money to travel to Hawaii."

"Yeah…I keep bringing it up because I've never gotten a reasonable answer from either you or Mom. Dad found the money to come. Where was she? Mom never once, not once, wrote a letter or called me. All the letters and calls came from Dad. And were you too busy traveling? You never wrote, called, or came either. Four months of hell living with excruciating pain from learning how to walk again, Henry, and not one word of encouragement from either you or Mom."

Henry had no answer. He knew he was being skewered and remained silent for a few moments, and then changed the subject.

"She's always been there for you, Ian, and you owed her that attention."

"Yeah…she helped me through my divorce because I was broke. But I paid back every cent. If I recall, she also helped you a number of times to pay your mortgage? Did you pay her back?"

"Yes, I did…in a way. I always paid for her trips and she always stayed with me. Besides, Mom never asked me for the money then, or now. Using your money for running her around was the least you could have done."

"If she is our mother, Henry, why would she have to ask? Why didn't you just offer it? She never asked me to repay the money or care for her—I just did. It's more than she ever did for me! I would have thought that would have been the least you could have done. You're the good son—so do it now, you cheap bastard."

Again, Henry had no retort other than, "I did my best to offer you advice on how to arrange for her care."

"Are you kidding me? I did all of that. Yeah, you gave some advice, which was mostly crap because you didn't have a clue how any of that worked. I had to learn on the fly, but yet you and Mom questioned every decision I made. Then, you came riding in like some white knight at the end of October to take her to Florida, and I was the one who cleaned up the aftermath with her doctors and the care providers. I had to take care of making sure all of her records and medications were transferred to Florida. I did it, Henry, just like I had to make all the arrangements for Dad's funeral. You strutted around like a peacock and sucked up sympathy like a vacuum cleaner, when you told everyone how difficult it was going to be to deliver the eulogy for your beloved father. But when the time came to perform, who was the one who delivered the eulogy? Me, you pompous blowhard. The big-time performer choked. You and Mom sat there bawling as you held each other."

In retrospect, even Ian was surprised just how much animosity he had developed for his mother and brother. *I am truly starting to hate them.* But his response was automatic. Ian opened his mouth and the words just fell out. What Ian didn't realize, or admit, was that he wasn't that different than Henry. He was just a different dog with a different bone.

And his volume ratcheted up: "You and Mom decided it was best for her to live in Florida. You never asked my opinion. So as far as I'm concerned she is your expense, because she is your mother—not mine. And you can put *your* in bold caps. Suck it up, big brother."

Henry was stunned. For years he had asked Ian why he was so resentful toward him and their mother. Years of multiple, rambling e-mails lecturing Ian on how much pain he was causing him and their mother with his shitty attitude, resentment, and defiance toward both of them. He pleaded, even begged for an answer, saying he was asking out of love as a big brother and a son. But he never got one. Now that he was getting his answer, he didn't know how to respond except to say, timidly, "She's our mother, Ian, and we both need to share in that obligation. We have a duty to help her."

Ian now screamed into the phone, "Listen the hell up, Henry. I've done my duty, with no help from you, thank you. She's your mother, not mine." Ian hung up.

"Now that you've decided to live in Florida, Gertrude, it would probably be a good time to update your will. I'll make sure it complies with the laws of Florida." James Farland was a solid attorney who entered his father's practice after law school and knew Gertrude and Larry through church, where Farland's father was also a member.

He took over the practice after his father died. Although semi-retired, he still maintained his relationships with his existing clients, leaving his oldest son to build the practice. Gertrude and Ian both trusted Farland because of their long-standing relationship; Henry trusted him because his mother did.

"Do you have any thoughts on how you wish to dispose of your estate at your death, Gertrude?"

"Yes, I do," she said with absolute certainty. "We have already gone through the house and I allowed the boys to take any items they wanted for themselves or their children."

"What about the property itself and your other assets, like your cash and investments?"

"Since the house is free and clear, I've decided to give it to Ian...now. Of course, I want to be paid for the furniture. All of my cash and investments I wish to give to Henry—now—with full Power of Attorney. He can use the money for my expenses while I'm living and whatever is left at my death, I will leave to him. I'm sure Henry will be prudent." Gertrude touched Henry's hand, although she looked straight at her attorney.

"Gentlemen, any thoughts?"

Gertrude snapped back authoritatively, "Their thoughts aren't relevant, James. This is my decision."

Ian sat there in total disbelief. *Son of a bitch. He wants me to help pay for her expenses when he's getting all the money. Cheap bastard wants to hold on to every penny of her money, to make sure he has as much of it as he can when she kicks. And now she wants me to buy used furniture? Are they kidding?* "Well...my thoughts are relevant, despite what my mother says."

"How so?" asked Henry.

"I'll tell you how so, Henry. You want me to help pay for Mom's expenses when you're getting all the money. And on top of that, Mom wants me to buy fifty-year-old furniture. How is any of that fair?"

"First of all, it's good furniture no matter how old it is, and I would think you would want it so you wouldn't have to buy any. Second..."

"I don't like it and I don't want it. It isn't worth shit to me and I have the money to buy my own. There's nothing there that is exactly antique quality. And if I'm moving in, I want it out so I can remodel the place to my taste. But just out of curiosity, Mom, what price did you have in mind?"

"What do you mean remodel it, Ian?" asked Gertrude with a shocked look on her face. "I don't want it remodeled." She paused then, stated with finality, "The house is fine the way it is."

Farland could see where this was going. With professional firmness he said, "Gertrude, if you are giving him the house and he is responsible for all of the expenses to maintain it, you don't have the right to tell him what to do with it. He can do with it as he pleases, assuming it's legal, and that means he can even sell it. Simple as that."

"Well, then, I will give him the house with the stipulation that he can not alter or sell it without my permission."

"Then forget it, Mom. No deal. I'll stay where I'm currently living, and you can do whatever you damn well please with it. Next!" Ian leaned forward and folded his arms on the table and remained silent. He'd been in sales long enough to know that when he made his pitch he shut up, and knew the first person who spoke—lost.

Everyone remained silent for what seemed like an eternity. Henry and Gertrude stared at Ian. Ian stared at Henry and Gertrude. Farland stared at his legal pad.

Gertrude clasped her hands so tightly together that her blue veins bulged, and set them in front of her. She looked directly at Ian and with a haughty voice said, "Fine, Ian, do with it as you wish. Just don't ask me or Henry for any advice or money."

"Trust me, Mom...I won't. Besides, Henry's advice is usually worthless and I doubt if he would part with any of the money." Ian shot his older brother a Cheshire Cat smile.

"There's still the issue with the furniture, Ian," said Henry.

"What about it? I told you how much I thought it was worth: nothing." Ian fixed his stare once more at his mother and brother.

This time Henry broke the silence. "We think it's worth at least two thousand."

"Where in the hell did you come up with that number?"

Gertrude slapped her right hand on the table and raised her voice: "It's what I want, Ian." She was growing more and more annoyed at Ian's perceived insolence. "It's either that or you keep it in the house. It's still my furniture."

She turned toward Farland. "Henry has always looked out for me, and cared for me, and has never asked me for a cent. But this one," she said, pointing and glaring at Ian, "is never satisfied, James, no matter how much I've helped him. I don't understand why he is being so unreasonable."

"I'll tell you both this one's idea," Ian said belligerently. "If you think the furniture is worth that much, then ship it to Florida and sell it yourself. See how much you get for it."

"That's not practical, Ian," said Henry, "and you know it. It would cost a fortune to ship it—probably more than it's worth."

"My point exactly." Ian decided he was willing to lose this battle in order to win the war. "So give me a real price, not what the two of you want."

Henry was infuriated at being called out, especially in front of his mother. "You know, Ian, Mom's right. There's no pleasing you. We give you a fair price for the furniture and you get a house for free…"

"Free? I'm paying for all the utilities, maintenance, and taxes. And you call that free?"

Henry stood up and slammed his hands on the table. His right hand shook as he pointed at Ian and shouted, "Look, you ungrateful piece of shit, I don't care what Mom or Jim says. You will either keep the furniture or pay what we want for it, and you will not change one goddamn thing in that house. It's Mom's house, and the house where we both grew up, and that's the way Mom and I want to keep it. Period."

Ian now stood and leaned over the table so that he was almost nose-to-nose with Henry. "Step off, Henry. You don't want me to live there. You want me to be the curator of the Gertrude Heller museum—but I refuse to live in some stinking museum. You're getting all the money and yet you still want more from me. If it's not covering her expenses, it's paying for worthless furniture. And don't ever refer to me as an ungrateful piece of shit, you cheap, money-grubbing bastard. Quit hiding behind your mother and fight your own battles."

"And you—" Ian said, returning the gesture and pointing at his mother as if his finger were a loaded gun, "you always found the time and money to go and see Henry at one of his shows, but you couldn't find the time or money to visit or call me, or write one miserable letter while I was laid up in the hospital, just like you couldn't find the time or money to visit your husband—my father"—pounding his chest with his right hand—"while he recuperated from his wounds. Neither you nor Henry lifted a finger to help me bury the man or give the eulogy. So, here's a news flash for both of you—you're Henry's mother, Gertrude, not mine. You never were, and never will be. You can take the furniture and the house and shove it up your collective asses. Stay the hell out of my pockets and out of my life." With a sweeping motion of his right hand he said, "You're fired—both of you, and I'm done here."

Ian turned to Farland. "Sorry, Jim," he said. "Now you see what I've been dealing with my whole life. Please don't include me in any more of these idiotic discussions. I have to get to work." He walked out of the room.

Farland had been here before with other families and knew when to play referee and intercede, and when to let events unfold unimpeded. This was one of the times, knowing the family history, to let events ebb to their natural conclusion.

"James… Please do something," pleaded Gertrude. "Get him back in here so we can finish these discussions. We have a flight to catch and I don't want it to end like this. They're brothers, and now they're behaving like enemies. Please?"

Farland sat back in his chair, clasped his hands together, and looked away as he chose the right words, as an attorney is supposed to do. Finally, he spoke, looking at Gertrude and Henry. "No, Gertrude, I won't. Ian is right, and you and Henry are wrong. Henry is getting in cash and investments three times what that house is worth, and yet the two of you are trying to squeeze every dollar from him. Ian shouldn't have to pay one penny for your expenses or for the furniture. You forget, Gertrude, I've been in your home and, although it's good furniture, I wouldn't give you anything for it. Both of you…let it go. You may think you're losing some money, but what you're really losing, Gertrude, is a son. And Henry, you are losing a brother. Is that what the two of you want?" Farland searched their faces for how his message was being received, but both Henry and Gertrude had turned away.

Long seconds passed. Then Gertrude again faced Farland. "James, you've been a good friend and attorney to our family, but don't ever forget who paid you. Who are you," she queried, leaning forward and wagging her right index finger at Farland, "to lecture Henry and me about family? We're not the ones who walked away—Ian did. Now do your job and settle this so we can go."

Farland closed his eyes and looked down, clenched his lips together, and nodded his head slightly. Then he looked up, slowly raised himself out of his chair, stood straight, smoothed out his tie, buttoned his suit coat, and walked to the door and opened it. He turned to Gertrude and Henry. "Friend and attorney to your family aside, Gertrude, don't ever think you can come in here and lecture me on how I do my job. I'm not going to charge you for this meeting, because I know you would just try to haggle with me as you did with Ian. In return, I'll consider this meeting, and our relationship, terminated—indefinitely. Gertrude. Henry. Good day." Farland, too, walked out of the room.

On the ride to the airport, Gertrude asked Henry, "Why is Ian so angry at us? What did we do to deserve this? When did all of this start, Henry?"

"I truly don't know, Mom. I wish I did. Don't worry, I'll talk to Ian. Remember, I'm his big brother and Ian will listen to me. He'll eventually come around."

8

I Thought Death Would Be Fun

"Hey, D. I've been looking all around for you."
"Well, you found me."
"Nice to see you, too! What's wrong? You look depressed."
"I'm not depressed, Sasha. I just don't like all this waiting."
"Waiting for what?"
"My mentee. It's always the same... Hurry up and wait."
"That's the way it is here. I thought you would be used to it by now."
"I'm not. And I thought death would be fun. This is work."
"Who is it?"
"Who is what?"
"Your mentee. My God, you *are* in a foul mood. Perhaps I should just go, and find a nice pile of snow to play in and leave you to wallow in your self-pity."

I died almost six years ago, close to my thirteenth birthday. Not bad, given my life expectancy was twelve to fourteen years, on average. I split the difference. Sasha beat the average when she died at age fifteen.

She's my mentor, and has become my friend. Sasha is patient, kind, but tough—sort of like a female drill sergeant—and has always been there to pull me through the rough spots. The best part is that she's a Siberian husky, like me, only copper and white. I'm black and white, much like my personality. She has brown eyes. Mine are blue. She gets me, and likes me…mostly. And then there are the other times.

Sasha is what we call an Old Soul. And it's not because of the age at which she died, but because of how long she's been here, at Here. Now that I think about it, I'm not sure how long she's been here. I've never thought to ask her. All I know is it was way before my time.

"I'm sorry. Don't go…please."

Sasha laid down beside me. "Okay, Dakota. But promise me you'll be in a better mood."

"Fine. I promise. Really." I gave her a sheepish smile.

"So who is your new mentee?"

"A boxer, from Brooklyn."

"Boxers are good. I've never had any trouble from a boxer. Dalmatians, on the other hand, are a real pain. Bunch of know-it-alls, and nasty. But that's a story for another time."

"But this boxer is different. I don't know what to do. And why can't they ever give me a husky?"

"Because that's not how it works now," she said, and shot me one of those "Why are you even bringing that up?" looks.

"But you mentored me, and we're both huskies."

"You know they've changed the rules. They no longer want the mentor to be of the same breed as the mentee."

"Always new rules. What was wrong with the old one?"

"Nothing, as far as I was concerned. And I didn't say I agreed with it, or even liked it, especially after all this time. But I suppose they have their reasons."

"And you never asked them why?"

"No, I didn't. Because when I agreed to be a mentor, as you did, we also agreed that their rules were final. I'm not one to buck authority. Not like some whom I know." She gave me a playful grin. That always meant "Let it go, because I don't want to talk about it any more."

"So, tell me, what is it about this boxer that's bothering you?"

"He's only a pup. Not even two."

"Oh..." Sasha said, pursing her lips and looking away.

"I don't like the sound of that. What does that mean?"

She didn't answer the question. Instead, she asked, "How did it happen?"

"He ran out of the house and into the street. He lived in Brooklyn. Need I say more?"

She took a deep breath, then asked, "I'm guessing you've never mentored a pup before."

"You have a keen sense of the obvious."

"You know, Dakota, I'm only trying to help, and I really don't need the attitude. You always get this way when faced with something new. If you want my help and advice, then I'm more than willing to give it. But if all you're going to do is keep throwing these smart-ass remarks at me, then you can find another mentor. There's no rule saying you have to stay with me. Just say the word, pal. I'll even put the transfer papers in for you! What's it going to be?"

I got up and started to walk away. Then I turned and barked, "No. I've never mentored a pup before and I don't know what to do. There. Are you happy?"

Sasha just stared at me. She knew I had more to say, and allowed me to vent.

"I had a full life, like most of the other dogs I mentored. I knew—they all knew, deep down, that our time would come, even if we didn't readily accept it. But a pup?" I couldn't finish the sentence.

She got up and strolled over to me. "It's not fair. That's what you wanted to say? Right?"

"Right! No, it's not fair, and I thought Here was supposed to be fair."

"Do you really want to have a discussion on 'fair,' or do you want to know how to handle the situation? If it's the former, then I'm afraid you're not going to be of any help to your mentee, because there is no good answer to that question. I know that, and I know you know that. We've had that discussion before."

Sasha was right. We had had that discussion. But it wasn't about me crying foul that I was here. It was about the timing of my departure from There. I left, and not of my own volition I might add, when I believed my owner—my friend—needed me the most. I was ready. He wasn't. I've come to accept my new state—more or less. He still struggles with his.

"Yeah. You're right. We've had that discussion before."

"But if it's the latter," she continued, "then I can help. Which discussion do you want to have?"

"I want…no, I need your help. Have you ever mentored a pup?"

"Many times. When you've been here as long as I have, it's inevitable."

"Speaking of length of service… Just how long have you been here?"

"Let's just say it's been from almost the beginning of our breed."

"What? A couple hundred years or so?"

She rolled her eyes, and said, "You really should brush up on the history of our kind, Dakota."

"Oh? Look who's copping an attitude now!" I responded.

"Okay. That was uncalled for. Most dogs don't know how long their breed has been around. The only reason I know it is because I was there when we finally came into our own."

"So, how long has it been?"

"You wouldn't believe me if I told you."

"Try me."

"Almost three thousand years."

I stood there, flabbergasted. My tongue fell out of my mouth—and if you know anything about huskies, it's a very long tongue. I thought, *Is she kidding? Or is she just trying to impress me?*

Sasha caught the gawk, and said, "See. I told you that you wouldn't believe me. But it's the absolute truth. I've never lied to you, Dakota."

Then her tone grew somber: "It seems like an eternity. There were times when I wished I could die again. If you think death isn't fun, try immortality." She let out a sigh. "But such is our fate. That's why I wanted to become a mentor. I figured that's how I could be of use: to have a positive impact, to help others adjust." Then she gave the biggest smile. "Even rock heads such as yourself."

We both howled with laughter for a few moments. But I still had the matter with the pup, and still needed Sasha's advice.

"How do I handle it?"

"Well, there's good news, and bad news. Which do you want first?"

"Give me the good news."

"Wrong choice. I have to start with the bad news."

"You always do this to me. You give me a choice, and then do what you want anyway. Why the pretense?"

"Because you have yet to learn that you can demand that I start with *your* choice. In short...you allow me to do it to you. But in this case, you wouldn't understand the good news, unless I explained the bad first. Sounds reasonable, doesn't it?"

"Sure. Sounds reasonable." *I can never argue with her whenever she says that. If I do, then she wants to know what's not reasonable. It's just not worth the effort.* "Go for it. Hope you don't mind if I lie on my back while you're explaining. I have an itch."

"If that's what will hold your attention, then I'm good with it. Scratch away." She continued: "Okay, the bad news. Pups are very confused when they get here. Some come into their own sooner than others, but the vast majority doesn't even realize what they are."

"What do you mean?"

"I mean they don't even realize they're a dog. They haven't developed their own personality—their own identity."

"How can they not know they're a dog?"

"How much do you remember when you were that age, Dakota?"

Good point! Not much. I didn't know what I was. The only thing I remember—vaguely—is that I had run away from my first family and found myself confined in a cage, in a large room, with a lot of other creatures that kind of looked like me. I seemed to be the youngest, and none of the others wanted anything to do with me. They all appeared to be resigned to some unknown fate. When I asked where I was and what was going to happen to me, they just shook their heads and said, "You'll see." I felt so alone and helpless. I felt abandoned. In retrospect, to say I was scared would be, well...a gross understatement.

After a while, I was moved to another room. The others didn't say a word. They all seemed to know something I obviously didn't. But they weren't sharing, and I didn't know how, or what, to ask.

Then, my friend...Allen—yeah, that's his name, Allen—came along. The others looked even more despondent because no one had come for them. I could have gloated, but I didn't. I wish Allen could have taken all of them.

"Not much, Sasha." I didn't want to tell her what I experienced. It was too painful. But I got her point.

"May I continue?"

I knew that wasn't really a question. "By all means. Please do."

"Thank you," she said and raised her eyebrows. "So, being confused, you have to allow them more time to adjust—to see for themselves that there are others like themselves. They may not immediately make the connection, but trust me, they start to figure it out.

"And then, they have their mentor. In this case, you! You're the one who has to inform this pup what he or she is, and help them to find their own identity. That's why your task is so very important. And that's why you *cannot* bring fairness into the mix. Pups are confused enough. They just don't have the intellect to digest that concept."

Neither do I.

"They can barely grasp the basics of what they are."

She saw me staring into the void, then asked, "Are you listening?"

I came back to her. "Yeah. I'm with you."

"You don't seem to be. What's on your mind?"

"Nothing." Although Sasha knew that wasn't the truth, she didn't pursue the question. The fairness thing was still plaguing me, and I believe she knew it.

"We're clear on the fairness issue? I mean...really clear?"

She truly gets me. "Yes, Sasha," I sighed. "I'm good with it." I wasn't, but she also knew that I would follow her advice, because I trusted her. "Okay," I said, and asked, "So is there a good-news side to this?"

"Yes, there is. But we're not there yet."

"More bad news?"

"Just one more point. Then we can move on."

"No rush. Take all the time you need. I mean, that's the one thing we have plenty of. Right?" I rolled my eyes.

"More so than my patience with you! I honestly don't know why I stay with you."

"Because you love my wit, boyish behavior, and good looks?"

"That wasn't a question," she said sternly.

I knew it wasn't, but I also knew which of her buttons to push.

"Now, where was I?"

"More bad news."

"Yes, more bad news. But it isn't as bad as the first one."

She's the only one I know who can assign degrees to bad or good news. What creativity.

She continued. "Pups, as you well know, are not very disciplined. It's just their nature. They have very short attention spans—like some older dogs I know." Sasha gave me another one of her looks.

"Speaking of short attention spans... Sorry. I can't seem to get rid of this itch. But I'm still listening." *I hate when this happens. It's always at the worst times. Oh well. Such is a dog's life.* "You were saying?"

"What I was attempting to explain, before I was so rudely interrupted, was that you have to be patient with pups. Repetition is key, and vital. Remember: they will *always* be pups. That will never change, as they will never grow older. But they do have the capacity to learn discipline, limited as it may be, depending on their arrival age."

Sasha watched me roll around on my back, my tongue hanging

out, with an ear-to-ear grin on my face, as I ruthlessly annihilated that itch. She added, "Then again, learning discipline is not age-dependent," and shook her head. "How old did you say this pup is?"

"Not sure. All I was told was that he is less than two. They never tell me any details about my mentees. Why is that?"

"Because those details could cloud your judgment—make you less objective. You're told what you need to know, and no more. You know that as well, smart boy. Besides, what difference would it make if you knew that he was one, or one and a half, versus two years old? He's a pup—that's what's important. You need…no, you must develop your observation skills and tailor your teachings accordingly. Sounds reasonable. Right?"

There she goes again! "Yeah. Right, Sasha. So, is the good news anywhere in your lecture?"

"This is not a lecture," she said in a lecturing tone. "I'm desperately trying to help you. This is mentoring instructions and insights 101. How did you ever make it this far as a mentor?"

I stood and shook myself, finally relieved of that pesky itch, and looked squarely at her. This time, I answered her with force: "If you have to ask that question, then you better take a good, long, hard look at who mentored me!"

Sasha looked stunned. She had never heard me raise my voice to her, or really push back. I didn't wait for an answer before I continued, "Despite *your* obvious lack of mentoring skills I've become a great mentor. Recount to me one time, just one time, you have ever heard of any complaint from a mentee of mine, or from those in authority! Well, can you?"

Sasha lowered her head, tucked her tail between her legs and said, "No, Dakota, I can't." Then she regained her composure. "But that doesn't mean you know everything. You've been doing this, for what, six years? I've been doing it for thousands, and I still learn with each mentee."

"I never said I knew everything. I admit it. Otherwise, I wouldn't have asked your advice on how to handle a pup. And don't twist my words or attempt to spin this. You're the one who implied that you were the All Knowing. You always have to come across all high and mighty. I'm surprised you don't ride around on a horse! And one would think that after several millennia, you would have this down pat!"

I was at a full run, and didn't let up. "And why is it always some competition with you?"

"What's that supposed to mean?"

"It means that no matter what we discuss, you always have to compare—to show that what you've done is better," I said, and mimicked her voice in an unflattering way, "'You've been doing this, for what, six years? I've been doing it for several thousand.' That's what I mean!"

Sasha's face wore an expression that I had never seen. It was a cross between being righteously indignant and off-the-chart pissed. She got in my snout and snarled, "You are such a child, Dakota. You've learned nothing, and never will. Pups have more intellect than you. The only difference between you and them is that you're in an adult body! But that doesn't make you an adult. It just makes you a big baby. There is no competition. You're no competition, believe me. And why do you always have to buck a system that's worked for, well, an eternity?"

"Thaaaat's right. Anyone who dares to question anything around here, or especially *you*, is considered a recalcitrant malcontent. Everyone in authority, Here, always believes they know what's best. Well, here's some bad news for you, Sasha: *They* don't know, and neither do you. You've obviously accepted all of this, but I haven't, and never will. I don't belong here. I never asked for any of this, and neither did Allen. You've never once asked me how I felt about leaving him. Not once!"

She wasted no time in her retort. The level of her voice matched mine: "None of us asked for this, Dakota. I know I didn't. And there were so few huskies when I came here, I felt like an outsider. Breeds didn't exist then like they do now. The other dogs, most of them wild, looked at me like I was some kind of freak. If there was anyone who felt like they didn't belong, it was me. And no one cared how I felt. You're right. It isn't fair. The only thing fair about all of this is that we all got here the same way.

"And I know you don't want to hear this, but I didn't ask you how you felt because it was irrelevant. It wouldn't...have changed...anything. Nothing! I mean, what would you have said? That you missed him? That you left too soon? Each and every one of us could have said the same thing. But nothing would have changed. We were here. And Here is final."

I heard her words, but it didn't change how I felt in the least. I took a deep breath and lowered my voice. "I thought you were more than a mentor to me, Sasha. I thought you were my friend."

I showed her my tail and walked away. Then I turned back. "I'm done with mentoring. I'm done with this place. And I am most certainly done with you. If you know so much, then you handle the pup!"

As I walked away, she said in a muted but commanding tone, "It doesn't work that way. And I know you know that. You can leave me. You can quit mentoring. You can have nothing to do with this place or those in it. But you can never leave Here. Death may not be fun. Maybe it's not supposed to be. Then again, maybe it's just a state of mind. It doesn't matter whether or not you accept it. It just is. Either way, it's forever."

That word *forever* made me stop. I turned again to address my brown-eyed mentor. "Although I knew better, for some foolish reason I thought that's what I would have with Allen. That's what I wanted with Allen. I've tried to stop thinking about him. And for a while, it seemed to work. In fact, for a moment during our discussion, I struggled to remember his name. Now this pup thing has made me deal with it…again."

I paused, looked down, and then whispered to the ground. "I'm never seeing him again, am I?"

Sasha's tone softened. "You will, eventually, Dakota."

"When?"

"When it's his time, and not before. You just have to be patient. Time doesn't seem to matter here. It's just a reference point that *we* assign. And please don't ask me when that time will be, because I don't know."

"I've never seen people here."

"They're here. We just don't usually mingle with them. But you will when Allen comes."

"How do you know that?"

"Because I believe he wants to be with you."

"Will I see you again when I'm with Allen?"

"If you want to. I know I would like that very much. But it's your choice. It's always been your choice, and always will be."

"I've never seen you with a person. Why is that?"

Sasha lowered her head, collapsed to the ground, put her paws over her eyes, and started to cry. I had never seen her cry before. In fact, I've never seen any dog cry before. I ran over to her. "What's wrong? Why are you crying?"

"Because no person has wanted to see me, that's why. You have Allen. I have no one!"

I could feel the emptiness. Thousands of years of stark loneliness. It broke my heart. *So long without a person to love you.* Then: *How could no one ever not want to see her? Not one person? How could anyone forget about her? Sasha is the best. Surely there must have been at least one person who saw that in her?*

I couldn't take it any more; I couldn't stand to see her in this much pain. As angry as I had been, the emotion passed so very quickly. There's something about Here that won't allow any of us to stay angry.

"You have me. You always have, and always will. I could never leave you, even if I'm with Allen. And if he doesn't want me, for some reason, then just know we will always have each other, for better or worse," I said, and I licked her nose. "Besides, how boring would it be for you if you didn't have a rock-headed, recalcitrant malcontent to keep you on your toes?"

She dried her eyes with one of her huge paws, and said, "Very boring, Dakota. Very, very boring."

We howled with laughter once again.

And perhaps she was right. If I'm here and can't be with Allen—at least for the time being—then I might as well make the best of it. Mentoring isn't my dream job, although I suppose there is some saving grace in the deed. Now, being part of a sled team…? That would be a dream job! I should talk to Sasha about who to contact. She has a lot of pull around here—no pun intended.

"Sasha?"

"Yes?"

"You were going to tell me the good news of mentoring a pup—if you're still willing, of course."

"Of course I am. And thank you for those kind words."

"I meant every word. And I'm sorry for snapping at you. You didn't deserve it."

"Yes I did, Dakota. I suppose I do get all high and mighty at times, and want to show everyone how much I know. I miss not having a person care about me as much as Allen cared about you. And this pup thing, as you called it, brought it to the surface. Truth be told, I've always been a bit envious of you and your relationship with Allen."

"Really?"

"Really."

"Huh. I never would have thought that. Well, I'm sure Allen would be your friend too, when he gets here."

"You think so?"

"I know so. Now, what's the good news?"

"The good news is that since they're so young, pups haven't formed any real bonds or attachments to their families. We become their family. They're very open to new environments, and they are very giving. They want to please. Just make your lessons playful, and they'll respond."

Family. Allen and I had had a big family. I loved the children and they loved me. We constantly played together. Allen's wife? Not so much. We were all together for about five years. Then Allen left. His wife said, "And take the dog!" She didn't even use my name.

The children saw me from time to time, but it was never anything regular. After awhile, they stopped coming to Allen's new place. We had very little company. Allen and I were alone, together. But we were never lonely.

No matter how tough it got for Allen, he always put me first. I once heard him say to someone on the phone, "I need to buy food for

Dakota and me. But after I pay the bills and the rent, there won't be enough money left over to feed both of us."

The person on the other end of the conversation must have asked a question. Allen responded, "I feed Dakota. He's my responsibility. I'll make do."

Things slowly, but eventually, got better for Allen. He had more money, and we moved to a nicer place. I started to believe it would be that way for both of us, forever. But then I got sick.

We were at my doctor's office and I heard him say to Allen, "It's just a matter of time, pal. He may be around for another month, or maybe six. I just don't know. My advice is to enjoy him while he's still here."

I didn't understand what he meant when he said it was just a matter of time. Let's face it: A dog's sense of time is beyond human comprehension. It was beyond mine, and still is.

Then the doctor got down on one knee and looked into my eyes. He said to me, "And you enjoy Allen for as long as you can, buddy," and rubbed my head.

The time thing still confused me, but I didn't need my doctor's advice to enjoy Allen's company. We did enjoy each other for a few more months—at least it seemed like a few months. Perhaps it was longer, or not.

Then one summer day, while he was taking me for a walk, my legs buckled, and I slumped to the ground. I was scared. But what scared me most was the look on Allen's face. He must have seen the fear in my eyes.

Allen sat by my side, and stroked me as he talked. His voice was comforting and encouraging. After a while, I regained my strength and stood. I managed to walk home with Allen, but I felt so weak.

He got me into his car, and drove me to my doctor's office. I always liked going for rides, but I wasn't enjoying this one.

When we got there, I heard the doctor and Allen whisper. Then Allen took me for a walk. It was my last walk with him.

He brought me back into the office and apologized to me for not giving me an easier life. Then Allen said he loved me, kissed me on my nose, and rubbed the back of my ears. Next to scratching my own back, having my ears rubbed was the best. That's when he said goodbye to me.

A young girl came in, gave him my collar, put on a different leash, and led me away. I looked back one last time at Allen. I wanted my eyes to speak to him, to tell him he gave me a great life, and that I wouldn't have traded it, or him, for anything. Mostly, I wanted to tell Allen how very much I loved him.

He must have read my eyes, because Allen gave a sad smile and said, "I love you, too, Dakota. We'll be together again, I promise." I knew that to be true, because he always kept his promises to me.

The next thing that happened was that I was here. Sasha came up to greet me. I don't know what I would have done without her.

As I reflected on my life, and the end of it, I understood what Sasha was so passionately trying to explain to me.

"I get it. I'll be his family. The pup deserves it. And I'll keep my promises to him. You can count on it."

Sasha cocked her head, raised her eyebrows, and said tenderly, "Where did that come from?"

"Family's important. I had one, and you're my family now. The pup needs to have one."

"Perhaps I did a better job at mentoring than we both thought…huh?"

"Don't get a swelled head. You did an okay job. I'm just a slow learner at some things, but I eventually come around." I gave a quick half-grin.

At that moment, we both heard a small bark, and turned. About twenty feet from us stood the pup. He was a handsome guy—tan and white—and wagged his stubby tail wildly. The pup couldn't have been more than a foot tall.

I walked slowly toward him, stopped, and then said, "Do you want to come over here, or should I come to you?"

"Who are you?"

"My name is Dakota, and this—" I said as I turned toward Sasha, "is Sasha. What's your name?"

"Where am I?"

"You're at your new home. We call it Here. Do you have a name?"

"Of course! We all have names."

Sasha gave me a "How does it feel dealing with a smart-ass?" look. *She has a look for almost every occasion. They're mostly directed at me.* I ignored it, and asked the question again. "What's your name?"

"Oscar. My name is Oscar. And what am I doing here?"

"I know you have many questions, Oscar, and I will answer all of them in due time, I promise. Oscar's an interesting name. Do you know how you got that name?"

"Yeah. Eduardo gave it to me."

"Who's Eduardo?"

"The man who cared for me. I lived in his home."

"But do you know why he gave you that name? I believe I do."

Oscar moved cautiously toward Sasha and me. "Are you going to hurt me?"

"No, Oscar! No harm will ever come to you here. Did Eduardo harm you?"

"No. He loved me and took me everywhere with him. I had a nice warm bed, and plenty of food. Where's my bed and food, and where is Eduardo?"

I needed to change the subject. This was not the right time to answer those questions. I asked again, "Do you know why Eduardo gave you that name?"

Oscar inched closer. "No. Why?"

"Because you're a boxer."

"A what?"

"A boxer. That's your breed."

"What's a breed?"

"The family of dog you come from. You do know you're a dog, don't you?"

Oscar's eyes grew wide. There was now a determined look on his face, and he walked quickly and purposefully right up to me and said, "Of course I know I'm a dog! I mean, do I look like a cat to you?" He faced Sasha. "Are you any smarter than he is? Is this what I have to deal with *here*—wherever Here is?"

I had to bite my long tongue. *Ow! That hurt!* Meanwhile, Sasha marshaled up all her willpower to contain her laughter. Then her maternal instincts kicked in. She laid down to get eye-level with Oscar.

"Oscar…please come to me, and lie down. I need to share a few things with you."

Oscar dutifully settled down in front of Sasha. "Yes, Sasha," he said sweetly. "What is it?"

"Well, first of all, know that both Dakota and I have your best interest at heart, just as Eduardo did. And we promise to answer every one of your questions. You're a smart dog, and I know you'll answer some of those questions yourself."

"You bet I'm a smart dog," he said, and looked over at me with a puppy scowl. "I heard the teacher at my school tell Eduardo I was the smartest student in her class. I can shake hands, roll over, sit, stay, and fetch. Wanna see?"

"Sure," said Sasha, at which Oscar demonstrated each one of his lessons with great proficiency and pride.

"Pretty good, huh?" he said.

I had to chime in with my two cents. "That was excellent, Oscar. I can see why you were the smartest student. It's as good—" then, catching myself, "no, it's better than I can do. My apologies for questioning your intelligence."

Oscar's mood changed, and he came over to me. "That's okay, Dakota. You didn't know me. What I said to you was rude. Eduardo wouldn't have approved of that behavior. I'm sorry. Shake?"

"No apology necessary. But I accept. Shake."

Then he surprised me with his question. "So, why did he name me Oscar?"

"Well, you're a boxer, and there are people who box for a living…"

Oscar cut me off. "Oh yeah! I used to watch them with Eduardo on this screen in our home."

"The television."

"What?"

"That screen is called a television."

"Whatever, Dakota."

Sasha looked away.

"So what does boxing have to do with me?"

"One of the best boxers ever is named Oscar De La Hoya. Very famous. I believe he named you after him. It was quite clever, actually."

"You mean I'm named after a famous person?"

"I believe you are."

"Then…" Oscar's wheels were turning. "That makes me famous. Right?"

Sasha and I looked at each other and smiled. We responded in unison, "It does, Oscar."

"Wow! That means Eduardo is pretty smart, too?"

"You bet," I nodded. "He's a smart and loving person."

Then, just as quickly, Oscar's smile turned to a pout, and he asked the question both Sasha and I hoped he wouldn't. "Where is Eduardo? When can I see him?"

I wanted Sasha to answer, but she remained silent. She knew that if I was to be Oscar's mentor, I would have to deal with these tough questions. I took a deep breath and said, "Eduardo is still at your old home, Oscar. But you will see him again at the right time. You just have to be patient. Believe me, he wants to see you again. Eduardo wants to be with you, as much as you want to be with him.

"How do you know that?"

"Because I also have a friend I'm waiting for. A friend who also wants to be with me. We all come here when it's the right time. This is your time. Eduardo will have his."

I could see Oscar struggling with my answer. Then, I thought of another way to explain it. "Did you ever race another dog, or Eduardo?"

"Always. I would beat all of them, especially Eduardo. Why?"

"Well, think of this as a race, and you won! You beat Eduardo again."

Just as quickly, his mood changed. "Wow! I won another race. That's great. So Eduardo will catch up to me soon?"

"Eventually. He's just a little slower than you. But he will catch up to you. Okay?"

"Okay, Dakota. Hey… Wanna race me? I bet I can beat you, too. You look old."

"Another day, Oscar. Another day. And I'm not as old as you think I am. I just look old to you."

He gave a bored yawn, then asked, "Can I go play now? There are a lot of things in this field I want to chase."

"Absolutely. Play away."

"Will I see you and Sasha again?"

"If you want to."

"I do. But how will I find you?"

I looked around, then spied a landmark. "You see that big tree over there?" I asked, pointing.

"Yep."

"Well, how about we meet there every morning just after the sun comes up?"

"I can remember that. That's when Eduardo always took me for my walks." He then asked in rapid succession: "How will I find the tree? How will I know when it's the right time? What if I get lost?"

"Just think of your walks when the sun rises and you'll find your way there at the right time. And you won't get lost. Sasha and I will always know where you are. Always."

"Sounds easy enough. I'm a smart guy. I'll figure it out."

Before I could respond, he ran off. Then, just as quickly, he rushed back to me, licked me on the nose, and said, "Thanks, Dakota."

"For what?"

"For being my friend." He padded over to Sasha, licked her nose, and thanked her as well.

"And Dakota?"

"Yes?"

"Could I just call you D? It's easier for me to say and remember."

"Sure. A good friend of mine calls me that."

"That makes me a good friend, too. Right?"

"Right."

"And you can call me O."

"Well, I think I'll stick to Oscar. It's what Eduardo wanted. Okay?"

"Okay. See you tomorrow," he said, and off he ran, jumping up and down in the field until he was out of sight.

"He's seems to be adjusting quite well, don't you think, Sasha?"

"As I said, he's a pup. They adapt very quickly."

"And Oscar's moods and questions changed so quickly. I never realized how short a pup's attention span was," I said before I started rolling around in the clover.

Sasha stood there staring at me.

"Whaaaat?" I questioned. "This feels good!"

"Apparently short attention spans aren't limited to pups," she said, grinning.

I stood and shook myself, looked at her, stuck out my chest, and said with pride, "And apparently I'm a pretty good mentor, if I must say so myself—thanks to you, of course."

"You're welcome."

I paused. "I really appreciate what you did."

"What did I do?"

"You got Oscar and me over the hump. I was losing him until you stepped in."

"It was just my maternal instincts, that's all."

"But I don't have maternal instincts. What do I do the next time that happens?"

"What you did this time. You made it a game. I thought comparing Eduardo's arrival to a race was brilliant."

"Really? Brilliant?"

"Really and truly. Oscar got it. You answered his question, and he moved on. In reality, you gave him the means for him to answer his own questions, and come to his own conclusions. And that's always more powerful."

"Perhaps I should try that for myself, Sasha."

"You already have."

"When did I do that?"

"Many times. You just never made the connection. More recently, when you answered your own question on fairness."

"When did I do that?"

"When you agreed to be Oscar's family, and that you would keep your promises. You knew what happened to him wasn't fair, but you were going to give to him what you had. You wanted to be fair with him. You decided to give of yourself, Dakota, and I couldn't have been more proud to be your friend than at that moment."

Sasha gave me a small bite on my snout, and licked my nose. It's the ultimate sign of affection between huskies.

"Thanks." I returned the gesture. "Do you think Oscar will ask that question again?"

"More than likely he will, and many more. But now you're prepared."

"Do you think he'll meet us tomorrow morning?"

"I'm sure he will. He's a smart pup and wants to learn. But more than that, he wants and needs a friend, more than he needs a mentor. Be his friend and you will not only gain his trust, but his love."

"Just like us?"

"Just like us."

"So, what do we do for the rest of the day?" I asked.

"Well, I'm sure we can find a snow pile to play in. Or we can take a nap. Pick one."

"A nap sounds great!"

"Wrong choice. It's the snow pile."

"No," I pouted and put my paw down. "I want to take a nap. You're the one who said I should demand to start with my choice. A nap is my choice."

Sasha gave me a puppy look, sighed, and said forlornly, "Okay. I suppose we can find a snow pile another day." And then she said just under her breath, "I could have sworn there was only one pup."

"Hey. I heard that," I protested; then I pondered her words. "Fine! The snow pile it is. Let's go." *This will never end,* I thought, shaking my head.

"You're the best, Dakota." Sasha nuzzled her head into my side.

She gets me. I smiled.

As we sauntered side by side in search of that snow pile, I had a thought: *My dream job.* "Hey, Sasha?"

"Yes, D?"

"Whaddaya know about sled teams?"

9

As If

"So...am I a replacement, or an addition?"

Only Christie had the courage to ask a question like that and not think about the consequences. She delivered it with the same deftness and precision as a gladiator finishing off an opponent. Her size, as she put it—"I'm five-foot-nothing. I'm fun size"— belies her ability to go in for the kill. One of her most endearing qualities, at least to me, is that she is fearless.

Christie was starting her senior year at Juniata College, which is located in the heart of central Pennsylvania. She asked that question without any warning halfway through our three-hour trip.

It was a fair question and one I'm not surprised she asked, given my correspondence with her earlier that year. In reality, I would have preferred she hadn't asked it. I thought about copping out and saying "both," but that would not have been the truth. Besides, I knew Christie wouldn't tolerate that answer. With her you're either in or out; yes or no; black or white—there is no middle ground.

Christie is the granddaughter of a woman I have dated on and off—mostly off—for the better part of six years. Her grandmother, Samantha, raised Christie from infancy after Christie's mother died at twenty-five and her father abandoned her. Samantha's decision to raise Christie was a seminal one; she had done this before when her first husband passed away at a young age, leaving her to raise their three girls alone—one of them Christie's mother.

Her surviving daughters weren't, and aren't, any help. One daughter has been institutionalized most of her life for mental illness, and has been and in and out of drug rehabs. The other is dangerous, even when she is on her meds. One look in her eyes, and I knew she would gut me like a fish with a butter knife, just to inflict maximum pain, the first time I pissed her off. I made sure that first meeting was the last.

Samantha dated, but none of the men stayed around long enough, nor showed enough interest, to really get to know Christie, and vice versa. That is, until I entered the fray. It was perhaps the third or fourth date I had with Samantha, when she finally felt safe enough to allow me to pick her up at her home. It was then she introduced me to Christie, who was just starting her junior year in high school.

She was in her room when Samantha called her to come down. Apparently Samantha told Christie I was stopping over, because she came bounding down the stairs with a sense of urgency and excitement like someone rushing to meet a long-lost friend. Christie's fair complexion blended seamlessly into her almost shoulder-length, naturally dirty-blonde hair, which appeared a bit unkempt. On her it looked charming. There was calm in Christie's almond-shaped, brown eyes, which I was surprised to find given the turmoil in her young life.

Before Samantha got out the introduction, Christie said in a perky voice, "Hi Ian, I'm Christie." She had a perfect smile, which highlighted perfectly straight teeth. I was about to say hello and shake her hand when she wrapped her arms around my waist and gave me the most intense, warmest hug. It was as if she was trying to crawl inside of me. The hug lasted at least three Mississippis.

I glanced over Christie's right shoulder at Samantha, who stood there with her mouth open. She looked like a fish in a tank that was about to be fed.

I gave Christie a polite hug and slowly pushed her away. She looked up, smiled, and said, "Great to finally meet you, Ian. Grandmum has told me so much about you." I was somewhat taken aback. I mean, how much could Samantha have told her about me, considering I had been dating her only a short while?

"All good, I hope?" I mumbled.

"Absolutely. She said you were a gentleman, funny, and handsome. I don't know about the funny part but it appears she was right about the other two. Hopefully, I'll get to see the funny part of you as well."

Fearless. That's when I first realized Christie had no fear saying what was on her mind. This was a girl who had a commanding presence in spite, or perhaps because, of all she had been through. I was both impressed and amazed, as I had imagined she would have been somewhat standoffish, given her history with the men in her life.

Again I mumbled, "Pleasure to meet you as well, Christie. Your grandmother speaks highly of you. In fact, you are the center of her online profile."

There was no response, other than, "Well, I have school work to do, and you two better get going or you'll be late for the movie." She said it with the authority of a mother ushering off her daughter after meeting her date for the first time.

"Yeah, it was great to finally meet you, Christie. Hopefully we'll meet again." I didn't know what else to say. Truth be told, I felt stupid and awkward, like a teenage boy who had just had his first kiss. Then, without another word, Christie gave Samantha a quick hug and kiss and bounded back upstairs with the same energy with which she came down.

"I suppose we better get going or we'll be late," I said to Samantha. "Mother has spoken." I smiled.

Once in the car Samantha looked straight ahead and never once glanced at me. It was like she was in a trance, as she didn't say a word the entire ride to the movie theater. I wasn't sure what was on her mind but hoped she wasn't pissed at me. Although I was pretty sure I hadn't done or said anything wrong, I wasn't entirely confident. With women, you just never know.

In the parking lot, I shut off the engine and sat there for a moment choosing my words. Finally, I found the courage to ask Samantha what was on her mind.

"Why do you ask?" answered Samantha.

"Because you haven't said a word or looked at me the entire way, which isn't like you. You've been sitting there like a zombie. Look, I don't claim to know you all that well, Samantha, but we seemed to have a connection. We both felt it from the first time we met." I paused, waiting for an answer that didn't come. So I asked, "Didn't we?"

"Yes."

"Then what's wrong? And don't say 'Nothing.'"

"You haven't done anything wrong, Ian."

"I didn't ask if I did anything wrong. I asked what's wrong. You've been in a trance-like state since we left the house."

Samantha started to cry. *Shit. It's only been what, three or four dates, and I already have her crying? That's a new record, even for me.* She turned toward me. *Here it comes.* "You're a great guy, Ian, but..."

"It's the way she hugged you."

I wasn't relieved by the answer. In fact I was terrified. Did she think I was some dirty old man—some kind of pervert? I blurted out in rapid fire with a terrified expression on my face, "Yeah, I didn't expect that, Samantha, really. I'm sorry if I did anything wrong. I really didn't hug her back. Did I do something wrong?"

Samantha touched my hand. "There's nothing wrong. You did nothing wrong."

"Then why are you crying?"

"Because she's never hugged any man that way. She rarely hugs me that way."

I have always believed I was an intelligent, perceptive guy. But now I was completely confused, which, I must admit, still comes naturally for me when it comes to women. "I'm not sure what you mean, Samantha."

Samantha went on to explain that she believed Christie was an empath, and that she saw and felt things others didn't. "She sees something in you, Ian. I believe she saw an aura around you and she was attracted to it." Samantha has always been into the cosmic realm.

I knew nothing about empaths, except for the one on *Star Trek: The Next Generation*. Not wanting to show my complete ignorance, as I figured that would come to light soon enough if we stayed together, I asked, "You mean, like a smell?"

"No, silly, a light around you."

I was relieved. "Do you see that light?"

"No, but I feel comfortable with you, like we've met before. Like in another lifetime. But Christie seems to instinctively know who is a good person and who is not. She obviously saw that in you…a good person, that is."

I wanted to say: "Dogs do, too," but thought better of it. So I came out with a clever statement: "We should go or we'll miss the movie." Brilliant; just brilliant.

I don't remember much of the movie or the dinner afterwards, because all I thought about was Christie's hug. I didn't even get those types of hugs anymore from my children. What did she see in or around me?

I excused myself from Samantha's invitation to come into the house after I took her home, saying I was tired. Actually I was afraid—yes, afraid—I might see Christie again, and I didn't want to repeat the hug experience. After I gave Samantha a quick kiss and a hug, I walked back to the car and drove off as fast as I could. For the next few days that hug preoccupied me and crowded out most other thoughts, like an overweight person who sits next to you on a plane and takes up every square inch of the arm rest. I avoided any conversation with Samantha outside of a few texts. I still wanted to see her, but not until I sorted out this hug thing.

I came to the conclusion that I, too, felt a connection with Christie, but it wasn't because I saw any light around her. Perhaps it was because of my estranged relationship with my daughters that occurred after my divorce—especially my youngest, who was only a few years older than Christie. Perhaps I was missing the same hugs she used to give me when I came home from work when she was a child. But my gut told me that wasn't the answer. For many years after my separation and divorce, I had no idea of who I was or had become. So it should have come as no surprise to me that I wasn't sure what I was feeling, let alone why.

Eventually, I came to understand what I was feeling. It was a sense of not belonging, and I have always suspected Christie felt she didn't belong to anyone either, other than her grandmother—and maybe even felt abandoned. I knew something about abandonment.

I was the sole survivor of an ambush on my river boat in Vietnam. For many years I believed I abandoned my crew, because I didn't join them in death.

I came to the belief that Christie might also have shared the same feelings because, when she was three years old, her mother tucked her into bed, read her a story, and kissed her on the forehead after saying "Goodnight," then closed the door, walked to the garage, grabbed the loaded handgun she had hidden, cocked the hammer, inserted the gun into her mouth, and pulled the trigger. A single shot. Christie never heard it, but has felt the effects from it ever since.

Christie was told that her mother just stopped breathing—and that is what she believed, until she found out the truth years later from the next-door neighbor's child, who blurted it out in an angry tirade. Samantha confirmed it. Now it was Christie's truth to deal with. She must have felt—and perhaps still does—that both parents abandoned her, with one going so far as deciding death was the preferable choice. I can't imagine how that must screw with a child's mind. Christie had to start over like I did, and find out where and to whom she belonged.

Belonging, or—more accurately—not belonging, was perhaps our connection. No auras, no cosmic intervention—just raw emotion.

"What do you mean?" I asked, glancing at Christie, then quickly turning my head back to the road ahead of me. In that briefest of moments, our eyes met. Her look said it all. I was playing stupid, but she wasn't having any of it. She then sat cross-legged, folded her arms across her chest, leaned back into the seat, and stared out her window into the forest that lined her side of the highway.

Over the years I have gained some insight into Christie, but it's been by accident. Just little things she has written in e-mails or said over lunches when she was on break from college. The one glaring insight was Christie's appetite for life. She attacked and devoured it like a cheetah that runs down its prey on an African savanna, and then savors its kill, leaving only scraps. Christie left only the scraps of her life for others to find and interpret, and they had to be satisfied with them. She always had to be on the move. Staying static was never an option. Sharks exhibit the same behavior.

She could also be very pragmatic and judgmental and didn't feel she had much, if anything, in common with other kids she knew, especially the girls. Christie felt they were mostly immature and naïve because of "the risky behavior" they took with boys. She only had a few friends and even fewer she could rely on—other than her grandmother and me. Christie would learn in time that this reality also applied to her then-boyfriend.

There is one thing that makes Christie go ballistic: She doesn't take well to broken promises—not that many of us do—but she has a visceral reaction to them. I believe she views a broken promise as another form of abandonment. Her now ex-boyfriend, whom she had dated since her junior year in high school up until this past summer, had broken a number of promises. One of them was when they were supposed to meet in Italy, where he was studying for a semester, while she was studying in England. She had saved her money to see him by scrimping when she could have used the extra money to enjoy herself. When he blew off the visit, I was told she was furious. Knowing Christie, a small nuclear detonation might have been a better description. Had he been in her presence, he surely would have been laid waste by the force of that explosion.

That was the beginning of the end of the relationship. It was shortly thereafter she told him they were through; simple as that. No tears. No drama. She got over the breakup faster than he did. I believe she was over it before she even told him. To Christie, he was just another person—with the exception of Samantha and me—whom she felt didn't care enough to get to know her. I'm convinced Christie doesn't want many others to really know her. That would leave her too vulnerable.

But it was over lunch one day when she was home from college, that all of my theories about her insecurities seemed to coalesce. She said she hoped to marry, but didn't want children. I asked her why. She squared her face, looked straight at me with eyes that could have shot a laser and said, "Because I don't, that's why." I have never heard anyone answer any question with such definitiveness and defiance. It was her way of saying: "I'm done with that question and you better be as well, because that's the only answer you're getting...ever." I will never ask that question again.

A letter I wrote to Christie about eight months ago may have been the genesis of her now-infamous question. Apparently Christie believed I kept a relationship with her to stay connected to her grandmother, and mentioned this to Samantha. Nothing could have been further from the truth; I hadn't dated Samantha in almost a year. This was another one of Christie's insecurities. She always had to make sure who was for real. It reminded me of my dog, who would sleep with his back against my leg just to make sure I was still there.

So I wrote, not giving away what her grandmother had told me. I felt ashamed, as it should have occurred to me that she might think that. It didn't, because I took her affection and her for granted. If I have learned nothing else over the years, it's that you don't take the affections of others for granted. I directly stated in that letter, *"My relationship with you, Christie, has nothing to do with your grandmother. Our relationship stands on its own. I will continue to treat you, and love you, as if you were my daughter."* But the "as if" was the rub. I could treat and love her as a daughter, but she would never be my daughter. Worse, I had no idea if that was what she even wanted because I never asked.

I didn't have the balls to say any of that to her in the letter, but what I did write was the truth, and I hoped she would accept it. She did, or at least pretended to, because she sent back a thank-you note of sorts. For the moment, I thought I had dodged the bullet, that she wouldn't press the issue. She didn't, until that ride back to college.

"You know what I mean, Ian," Christie said, speaking to the window. "Don't play stupid with me. I deserve better." There was a tinge of anger in her voice, mixed with the hint of a child's pout.

For almost eight months that question must have rattled around inside of her head just waiting for the right moment, the perfect time to pounce, and she found it in the car. Christie could not have planned it better, as I had no place to hide, physically or emotionally. I could not hide behind a letter where every word and phrase was carefully crafted to convey a thought, yet still not expose my vulnerability. It's not that what I wrote wasn't true; it was. But it didn't address the real reason as to why I felt such a connection to her. It was an act of omission, and I believe Christie instinctively knew that.

It was that hug. And although there were many hugs over the years, that first one was the most satisfying, and yet the most tormenting and terrifying, because it exposed my emptiness—my sense of not belonging. Unwittingly or not, she made me face it. I came to the conclusion that I was a coward, and she was the fearless one. She had faced, battled, and dealt with her demons. Christie was like a gladiator who went into the ring and believed she would always win.

"You're neither, Christie," I said as I looked straight ahead at the road in front of me. "Although I will always treat and love you as a daughter, you're not my daughter. We have no connection through blood or DNA, no history other than a chance meeting with your grandmother. You can't replace my daughters, and I wouldn't want to replace them. As much as my relationship with them pains and tortures me, they are still my daughters.

"Nor can you be an addition to my family, as I can't adopt you, and that's assuming you would even want that. Your grandmother has chosen to be your legal guardian and not adopt you, so you could retain your mother's name, be your own person, and carry on your mother's legacy. Yet you are an addition to my life, Christie—a wonderful and pleasing addition. I suppose we both have to settle for that."

I paused for what seemed an eternity. Then I said what really needed to be said—what I didn't say in that letter. "You're my second chance—my chance to get it right. Perhaps I am yours. Perhaps that is our connection, Christie—a second chance to belong."

Sometimes you just have to say what needs to be said, and let the chips fall where they may. That always sounded good on paper.

The silence that followed was absolutely deafening. Like being in the vacuum of space, where you can't hear yourself screaming or crying.

The balance of the ride to Juniata was reminiscent of my ride to the theater with Samantha almost six years earlier. Christie sat bolt upright in her seat, mouth clenched shut, looked straight ahead, and said not a word.

We arrived at the college and unloaded her belongings. It wasn't until we were finished and I was ready to leave that she finally spoke: "Grandmum gave me some money to take you out for lunch. Are you hungry? 'Cause I am." I thought twice about it. I was hungry, but more importantly, I knew if I said "no," that would have just been one more disappointment to add to the day.

Lunch was small talk and meaningless. For the most part we ate in silence. I always hated when I ate in silence. My mother would do that to me when I misbehaved, which was often.

I took her back to her dorm and walked her to her room. I said my goodbyes, and asked her to write or call if she needed anything. I outwardly cringed and mentally kicked myself after saying that, because I felt what Christie really needed, I didn't give her—an answer that would have made her feel as if she belonged. I expected the worst.

I walked out of her room and out of the dorm, and despaired that I might be walking out of her life. I didn't sense she wanted a hug, although I sure as hell wanted to give her one, and wanted one in return. *So much for a second chance. I've lost her, too,* I thought.

I started the minivan and stared out the windshield at nothing, and knew it was going to be a long ride home. Music was not on the agenda. That's when I was brought back to reality by the banging on my driver's side window. Christie's face was streaked with tears. I had never seen her cry. *Christ, I've now made two women in that family cry.*

I turned off the engine and got out of the car. Before I could mumble anything, she wrapped her arms around my waist with the same intensity and warmth as she did at our first meeting. This time, however, I didn't push her away. This time, I drew her closer and allowed her tears to soak my shirt as I stroked her hair—the same way I did when one of my daughters needed to be comforted.

No words were needed. We had both found our second chance.

10

Done with Crazy

Look at him. He comes in here on almost a daily basis for breakfast, takes the same seat, in the same booth, and places the same order. He always faces the door. It's a lingering habit from Vietnam. And I always wait on him. He's a good tipper and not demanding; he minds his own business. All he wants is to eat, read a book, literary journal, or some short stories in peace—maybe even scribble notes for a story he wants to write. And now this happens.

Suzanne and Janice are sisters and sometime lunch customers. Today they made their breakfast debut. We were busy, and the hostess had no choice but to sit them in the booth directly in front of Ian, with Suzanne facing him. Seeing this, I thought, *He is not going to be happy. I hope this doesn't affect my tip.*

Much to my surprise, Ian didn't seem to mind. He just went about his routine. I refilled his coffee and was about to take the ladies' orders, but they had already started with their drama du jour. I knew better than to interrupt; I just brought them their usual coffee and water for starters. They didn't acknowledge me.

"What's the problem with Kyle this time, Suzanne?" asked Janice.

"Same as always. He's so anal. God forbid I move one thing out of place, I get the rolling eyes and 'why can't you be more careful' look."

Sounds like Ian. He gives me the same look if I don't deposit his plates at precisely the correct spot on his table, or refill his coffee when it reaches the prescribed level in his cup. But I don't take it personally.

"Why do you get so upset, Suzanne? You've been seeing him for over a year, and it's not like you haven't noticed this before. I mean, isn't that one of the reasons you two don't live together?"

Suzanne broke into tears. Not uncommon with either one, but more so with Suzanne. Janice played the role of big sister and handed Suzanne her napkin. "What's the real problem, Suzy?"

Suzanne answered between sniffles, "He asked me for the key to his apartment—said it's not working for him anymore."

"And what caused that?" Janice asked matter-of-factly. "Something else must have happened for him to take such a dramatic step." She knew Suzanne.

"Well…I wasn't happy with his eye rolling incident last Friday, but didn't say anything. He asked me Saturday morning, before I left for work, if everything was okay."

"And you said what?"

"I told him nothing was wrong. But I sensed he wasn't buying it, because he remained silent. So to convince him, I said I would be over Sunday morning and we would meet our friends for breakfast. He seemed good with that response. We kissed and I left for work."

"And did you see him Sunday?"

"No. I texted him Sunday morning and said I had to clean the cat boxes and do some vacuuming around my place."

"YOU'RE SHITTING ME," Janice said, and quickly covered her mouth. The owner came over and asked Janice to keep her voice down, especially if she was going to use profanity, as there were children seated near them—not to mention Ian, who slammed shut the book he was reading. He was clearly annoyed.

Janice apologized and continued in a lower voice, but not low enough. My sole counter customer was a good eight feet away, and he was able to follow the conversation.

"How did he respond?" Janice asked.

"He immediately called me and asked if that meant I wasn't coming over at all that day. I told him I would try, but didn't think it would happen."

"And he said what?"

"He said he would go to breakfast without me, and that he was sure he could find something to do for the balance of the day, and hung up. Just hung up, without waiting for a response!"

"And then what happened?"

"I texted him back about twenty minutes later and said I would finish changing the kitty litter, take a quick shower, and come over. He wasted no time in texting me saying he had already made plans to meet up with other friends after breakfast, and wouldn't be available for the rest of the day. Can you believe it, Janice?"

"Yes, I can. And you can't blame him for that, sis. After all, you did blow him off. But how did you respond?"

There was dead silence which—to me, the other customers within earshot, and most especially Ian—was a relief.

Suzanne raised her head, and in a dismissive tone stated, "I sent him a text."

"And what did you say in this text?" Janice asked apprehensively.

All of us held our breath. I even saw Ian look up ever so slightly.

"Fuck you!"

Janice choked on her coffee. The counter customer put a napkin to his mouth to catch the food he was spitting up, and Ian dropped his fork, closed his eyes, and bowed his head, shaking it back and forth. I had to walk away. I can only imagine what Ian was thinking. He had been through a number of breakups. In fact, I've lost track of how many women had sat across from him. *But that was then, and this is now.* I'm sure the conversation he was hearing was nothing he hadn't heard before. He had been on both ends of that discussion.

"Christ, Suzy. No wonder he asked for the key back. Wouldn't you?"

Suzanne didn't respond directly to Janice's question. That didn't surprise me. "Well…I called several times Monday to apologize, but he wouldn't pick up and didn't respond to my voicemails. I sent him a text that night and asked if this meant 'keep in touch.'"

Janice waved me over to ask for more napkins.

"And how did he respond?"

"The next day he sent me the text asking for the key."

I suppose that was the "keep in touch."

"I called again, and asked him to call me at work. He sent another text saying no more conversation was necessary, and that I should mail the key back that day—and he emphasized 'today.'"

"And did you…mail the key back?"

"Yes. I figured there was no sense prolonging the inevitable."

Janice nodded in agreement. She asked, "Does he now have the key?"

"Yes, and he sent a text thanking me."

Janice hesitated asking the next question, but asked it anyway: "You didn't make a copy…did you, Suzy?"

Suzanne fired back, "No. I'm not a fucking stalker," and reached for the pile of napkins I had placed at the end of their table. There was a pause as she cried into the napkin and blew her nose. She continued, "Why can't I keep a guy, Janice?"

My counter customer mouthed to me, "I can't believe she just asked that question."

"I'm forty, and have never been engaged, let alone married. I mean, you and Scott are happy."

"Yeah, we are. But remember, he's number three."

Ian had been there, but only once…and that lasted thirty years.

Janice excused herself to use the restroom. I'm not sure if she really needed to use it. Perhaps all of this was too much even for her.

Ian was finished as well. As he was collecting his belongings, he happened to look up and crossed Suzanne's gaze. She stopped drying her eyes, glared and asked indignantly, "What are you looking at?"

Knowing Ian could be quite sarcastic, I'm sure he wanted to respond with "Nothing," but restrained himself. I was relieved. *Thank you, Ian.* Instead, he just stammered, "I'm sorry. I'm…" Then stopped. *Guess I'll never know what he was going to say. Perhaps he didn't either.*

Suzanne gave him an unforgiving stare, which Ian ignored. *He had been there before, too.*

I manned the cash register, and Ian paid his check. All he said was, "Trisha, I am so…done…with crazy." His quiet, resolute tone reassured me. I nodded.

He left me a bigger-than-usual tip.

11

Where's the Cow?

"Everything okay, ma'am?"

"Where's the cow?" Julia asked, contemplating the empty space.

The Deputy Sheriff's cruiser was parked directly behind her, its lights flashing. Julia stood there under the cloudless fall sky, back to the highway, arms folded across her chest. The rush of the passing cars and trucks rocked her slender frame, and blew her long hair in her face. She made no attempt to push it aside. The Deputy held his Smokey Bear hat on his head. He stared at her for a moment, then asked, "What cow, ma'am?"

"There was a billboard-sized cow THERE!" she exclaimed, motioning with her arm to where the abandoned road dead-ended at the highway, "with an arrow showing the way to the dairy farm. The road's still there, but where's the cow?"

Twenty years ago there was a pregnancy, and no husband. An argument ensued. Julia left. As she turned onto the two-lane blacktop—which then served as the main road into, and out of, her small town—she muttered to the billboard statue: "I hope I never see you again."

Decades passed. Her cousin wrote saying Julia's parents were ill, and that perhaps it was time to come home. They missed Julia, her cousin said.

It's been twenty years since I last saw or talked to them, Julia thought. *What's another few months?* That was six months ago.

The Deputy explained that there was a fire, and the dairy burned to the ground. Two people died. He asked, "Did you know them...the Cavanaughs?"

I thought I did. "Not really," Julia answered flatly. She stared into the vacant lot.

"Do you need any assistance, ma'am?"

I did, but not anymore. She turned toward the Deputy. "No thanks. I'll be fine." She gave an empty smile.

"Then I should be on my way, and so should you. It's not safe to sit here alone." The Deputy dipped his hat, walked back to his car and drove off.

Julia got back into her car and brushed the hair from her face. The young man in the passenger seat asked, "Is everything okay?"

"Not really, but it will be."

"Where to now?"

"Any place but here. And, Adam..."

"Yes, Mom?"

"Be careful what you wish for."

12

Solomon's Shadow

Cemeteries. I don't like being in close proximity to them, let alone being on the actual property. I have been too close to death too many times to feel comfortable in the presence of so much of it. But death always catches cheaters—except for my grandfather. He cheated death, through me.

On an unusually bright and warm fall day, I decided to visit my grandfather. Some people visit cemeteries out of love and respect for the departed. Some visit out of obligation, and others because of guilt. Mine was a mixture of those, plus fear. It's not much different than how we treat the living. I couldn't remember when I last saw him. He didn't get much company from those still above ground. Most of it came from his neighbors, and who knew how friendly they were to him—or he was to them.

My mother, who is in her nineties and a widow for the better part of fifty years, hasn't visited her father—my grandfather—since his death almost forty years ago. They never liked each other much—which always justified how I felt, and still feel about her.

When my grandfather died, my mother had him buried on the

other side of the cemetery from her mother—a grandmother I never knew. She blamed him for causing my grandmother's death at an early age from a broken heart. My mother always stated, sanctimoniously, that her mother deserved to rest in peace and didn't want my grandfather anywhere near her, even in death. Given that twisted and tortured logic, I always figured that if I died before she did, my mother would not allow me to be buried next to my father. She always blamed me for her husband's death, on account of my youthful misbehavior.

I walked to the older part of the cemetery where my grandfather was buried, with both trepidation and fear. A warm breeze picked up and scattered the dead leaves. They, too, had met their demise and found their resting place. So much death.

The leaves moved from grave to grave as if to pay their respects to their fellow departed. But strangely they stayed away from my grandfather's. Perhaps it was out of deference that they didn't want to disturb him, given the regal nature he exuded while he was living. Or perhaps it was out of fear. Nobody fucked with my grandfather while he was living, and I suppose some feelings are transmitted even after one's death. I didn't like him, but I respected—and yes—feared him.

The sun was now hitting the back of the gravestones so as to cast shadows, but the one emitting from my grandfather's seem to be longer and wider than the others. As I stood in front of his grave, the shadow completely engulfed me—just as it did while he was living.

I was sixteen when I buried my father. During February—a month before my birthday—he was diagnosed with cancer. In August, he died at the age of forty-six. The only person who truly believed in and loved me, and the only person whom I truly loved, was dead. At the cemetery, I broke down and openly cried in front of my family and friends. I had never before cried in front of anyone. In fact, I rarely cried at all, for any reason. As soon as the services ended, my grandfather put his large right hand on my left shoulder and ushered me away to a lonely corner of the cemetery. Ironically, it was the spot where he would eventually be laid to rest. Perhaps he knew something no one else did.

My grandfather turned me to face him. Without warning he slapped me across the left side of my face with that large right hand of his. He wasn't gentle about it. I stood about six feet and was an accomplished street fighter, but he'd slapped me so hard I spun around like a top. I was still looking down, stunned and rubbing my face, when I noticed I was standing in his shadow.

He gently placed the same right hand under my chin and raised my head. "Ian...look at me," he said firmly yet quietly in his now-faint Russian accent. When I looked up, I was amazed how tall he was and how he was dressed. I wondered why I never took notice before that moment. My grandfather was clean-shaven, six-foot-three, and stood ramrod straight, which made him look taller. He was wearing a crisp white shirt with a simple gray tie under his tailored, double-breasted, gray pinstriped suit with pleated pants. The hefty cuffs broke at just the right angle over his mirror-like shined black shoes. His white hair was parted on his left, and all were in perfect unison. They, too, knew their place. He had an air of royalty. It was fitting, because among his small circle of friends and to his clientele, he was king.

Even in his late seventies he had an athletic build and was imposing. He feared no one, and no one challenged his authority, especially his three children. In his younger days he was a prize fighter of sorts—the bare-knuckle kind where the winner was literally the last one standing. No ten-second counts in those fights. He took me to the gym and taught me how to fight. His advice on fighting was simple and straightforward: "Winning, Ian, means you are the last one standing. Always make sure the other guy doesn't get up." I always made sure the other guy didn't get up, or he at least thought twice before attempting it.

My grandfather stared at me for a moment, and then asked, "Did that hurt?"

"Yes, Grand-pop Sol."

"So why didn't you cry?"

"Because I've been in enough fights, and been hit enough times in the face that it doesn't bother me anymore. I've never cried, during or after a fight."

He pressed on. "Then why did you now cry in front of everyone?"

"Because I just buried my father, for Christ's sake. I didn't know I wasn't supposed to cry."

My grandfather gave a faint smile and nodded his head, then gave me the look I had seen so many times before when he was ready to impart his words of wisdom. "Don't you ever do that again, Ian. Ever. Never let anyone know what you are really thinking or feeling. And I mean no one, not even the people you believe you can trust. You never know when—not if—they will use it against you one day. If one hair on your head knows what you are really thinking or feeling, pull it the fuck out. Keep your own counsel. Your father did, and that's why he died with a full head of hair."

My grandfather emigrated from Czarist Russian to England as a teenager, and fought for the British in WWI, before arriving illegally in the United States. He did numerous odd jobs before eventually setting up shop in his chosen profession as a bookie. As visible as he was, he always managed to stay off the radar screen. The man had no use for any government and was his own authority. He did and said as he wanted, and never held a Social Security card or driver's license. My grandfather always kept his own counsel.

"Does that include you, Grand-pop?"

"Does what include me, Ian?" he asked, although we both knew exactly what I meant.

"People I trust who will turn on me?"

My grandfather dropped the smile, then tapped his right forefinger on his temple. "Trust only that people will do and say what's in their best interest. Always do what's in yours, Ian." He always did, and if someone benefited—and that included me and his children—it was purely by accident. He concluded his sermon: "People are unpredictable. All people." I knew better than to continue with that line of questioning. I had already received my answer.

He gave me a gentle slap on my right cheek. I didn't flinch. In a tone of voice I had never heard from him before, or since—almost a compassionate voice—he said, "Go mourn your father. When you're ready, come see me, as I have some errands for you. You know where to find me."

I always knew where to find him. If he wasn't at his home, he was at the playground card table with the same three men he had been playing cards with for as long as I could remember. They were all from Eastern Europe, and were a tough lot who kept their own counsel as well. My errands included running numbers for him, and now at age sixteen my best friend Mikey and I had become his collection agency. We reminded those customers who conveniently forgot their debts to him, to pay up. They knew who I represented, and absolutely did not want to deal with my grandfather. It was safer to deal with me.

My grandfather turned to walk away, then stopped and faced me. In the same tone he said, "God rest your father's soul, Ian. He was a good man. I would have rather had him as a son than your mother as a daughter." He paused, and then asked, "Do you know why your father died?"

"Cancer?"

"I didn't ask how, I asked why."

"I don't understand, Grand-pop. Why did he die?"

"Because he wanted to. He knew that was the only way to escape your mother, and God was merciful."

In the years between the funeral and my high school graduation, I had a number of run-ins with the police but was treated as a juvenile. The summer after I turned eighteen, I stole a car and was treated as an adult, with adult consequences. My mother's cousin—a prominent local defense attorney—brokered a deal with the judge. It was a simple offer: Serve honorably for four years in the military—and my sealed record would be expunged—or serve four years in the county prison and I would have a record forever. Given the Vietnam War was in full swing I almost opted for prison, but my grandfather convinced me the military would be the better option. The thought of continuing in my grandfather's business never crossed my mind. However, he still wanted one more errand from me. My grandfather always wanted one more errand.

Just before I entered the Navy, Mikey and I did one last collection for my grandfather. That's when a not-so-intimidated dead beat customer swung a bat at my head, like he was swinging for the fences after being served up a fast ball down the middle. Fortunately, Mikey warned me at the last moment and I ducked, but not before getting a two-inch gash in my scalp which required a dozen or so stitches. I didn't know it then, but that would be the first time I cheated death. There would be no more errands for my grandfather.

I served honorably for seven years, which included a combat tour on river boats in Vietnam. Once again, I cheated death when I was the only crew member to survive an ambush on my boat.

The balance of my career in the Navy was served onboard nuclear-powered, Fast Attack submarines. Why subs? Because of my grandfather. He would speak to me in Russian when he didn't want anyone else to know his business. His card-playing friends would always say, "Speak English, you commie bastard," and laugh. Knowing Russian was a winning lottery ticket during the Cold War, and submarines were in the thick of it. Events of a submarine, to the outside world, were on a need-to-know basis. The Navy—and the submarine crews—always kept their own counsel. I again felt a kinship with my grandfather. Even though he died while I was in the Navy, his shadow reached beneath the waves.

Through a moderately successful sales career and a not-so-successful thirty-year marriage—which ended in a nasty divorce—and the ugly aftermath, my grandfather's influence was never far from my conscious self. That slap, and the ensuing advice, did more to toughen me up for the real world than all of my youthful fights and my combat tour in Vietnam, combined. Although living my life on a need-to-know basis served me well working for my grandfather and on submarines, it didn't successfully translate into developing a loving and trusting relationship with my wife—and most especially—my three children.

I believe the only shadow I now cast, especially as far as my daughters are concerned, is one from that dark cloud of divorce which hangs over their heads. They are not terribly fond of me, in the same way my mother and grandfather—or my mother and father—were not fond of each other, and I am still not fond of my mother. I suppose some things, and most people, never change. It appears to be a vicious cycle. Fortunately my son—my oldest child—had the good sense to step out of whatever shadow I cast, which probably is why he and I have developed a good relationship.

The sun was setting and the air returned to a more seasonable fall chill. The shadow from my grandfather's gravestone was fading. I stood there wondering if I had the courage to finally step out of it. Strangely, I pondered how my grandfather felt about it and still feared his response.

For the longest time I took some perverse comfort believing his shadow was his way of protecting me—saying he loved me. As much as I feared him, what I now feared most was facing the sunlight alone.

13

Combustible

Grace and I met six months ago. Mutual friends who had been conspiring to get us together finally succeeded.

We decided to meet at a popular local diner for coffee. I arrived early and sat on the fake leather bench in the cramped lobby with the others who were waiting to be seated, nervously tapping my feet on the floor.

The anxiety of this first date must have also shown on my face. A middle-aged lady sitting next to me to my left asked, "Blind date?"

I turned toward her, sheepishly grinned, and answered, "Yes."

"That's how we met, almost ten years ago," she said, and motioned with her head to the man sitting to her left. The hostess called their name. As they stood, she looked back at me, smiled, and said, "Good luck."

I gave a half-hearted smile in return, and mouthed the word, "Thanks."

Although Grace and I had no idea what each other looked like, other than vague descriptions our friends had given us, we instinctively recognized each other when she walked through the door. She had a smile like Annette Bening, and that was all I could see.

It was six p.m., the height of the diner's dinner trade, but we managed to corral a window booth. Grace and I bonded and trusted each other immediately. We talked over coffee for five hours. I left the waitress a generous tip for allowing us to rent her table. Now in our sixties, we decided we didn't want to go through life alone anymore. Two months later, Grace moved into my apartment.

One night, as we lay in bed, Grace asked, "How would you describe our relationship, Lewis?"

She has a knack for asking these weighty questions at the most inopportune times. It's always when I'm ready to fall asleep. Somehow, she instinctively knows that's when I'm most vulnerable.

"What?" I asked incredulously as I rolled onto my right side to face her. She had already turned off her lamp. My eyes squinted as I tried to focus on her, aided only by the broken bands of light from the street lamp sifting through the blinds behind her.

"How would you describe our relationship? It's a simple question." The muffled sounds of midnight traffic rose from the street two floors below our apartment.

Perhaps for her the answer was simple, but not for me. I was no more prepared to answer that question in my sixties than when I had to answer it forty years ago in my twenties.

"Not at this hour, when I'm exhausted and want to sleep. And why would you ask that particular question now?"

"Because this is the perfect time to talk—when we're together and have no distractions."

She's right, partly. With our schedules, it's probably one of the few times we get to talk to each other. I still work a full-time, modified, second-shift job. I rarely get home before ten p.m. and, by then, I just want to vegetate. Grace is retired, but teaches both a day and evening English as a Second Language class on a volunteer basis.

"You mean other than attempting to get some sleep before I have to wake up in six-and-a-half hours?" I asked.

"Well, that's an hour longer than me. I'm up at five-thirty."

"That's out of habit and your choice, Grace, not mine. Good night," I said as I rolled back, facing away from the window.

"And where are you going?"

"Hopefully to sleep, please?"

"You're not answering my question, Lewis."

"I thought I just did," I mumbled into my pillow.

"I heard that, and it's not the answer I was looking for."

Lord, help me. Exasperated, I turned on my nightstand lamp, rolled over once again to face her—like a dog learning a new trick—propped my pillow up against the headboard, and sat upright. "Christ. You really want to know?"

Grace is a pebble compared to my boulder-like build. She inched closer to me, reclined, placed her left hand under her head as a prop, and said, "Yes. I really want to know. And don't bring Him into it. I asked you, and He's not going to help you answer the question." I'm Jewish. Grace is Catholic, and she doesn't take kindly to me using her Lord's name cavalierly.

"Why?"

"Why He's not going to help you?"

"You know what I mean, Grace. Why do you want to know?"

"Because by knowing what you think and feel, I believe we can make our relationship better, stronger."

"Okay. That's a valid point, I guess." I was doing my best to appease her.

That may have been her goal, but from what I know about Grace's past, I believe the question stems from insecurities about where she stands in a relationship. I struggle with those same doubts, as perhaps most people do when embarking on a new association, whether it's personal or business.

She's had two marriages. Her son and a daughter were from her first—which lasted only six years, and was fraught with her ex-husband's infidelities. The second was almost four times longer, and ended when she became a widow. That was seven years ago.

I had only one marriage, which endured longer than both of hers combined before I called it quits. With my ex, what I did was never enough. Never enough money, affection, attention. My worth, to her, was ultimately reduced to what I could give her. Our three children have the same mindset. My relationship with them is strained, at best.

Grace and I have shared morsels about our past relationships, her more than me. I've lived my life on a need-to-know basis; the truth comes out in dribs and drabs at my convenience. Perhaps—no, not perhaps—I *know* that was one of the many reasons my marriage ended in a heap of hot, smoking ash. I reluctantly shared that with Grace as well. She asked me to promise her that I would do better in our relationship. I said I would, and I always do my best to keep promises.

I've managed most of my insecurities: not being a good enough provider or father and husband, which stem from my previous marriage. There are probably also a few that I'm not conscious of, or willing to admit, but I still feel their effects. Those are buried so deep that some shrink attempting to excavate them, like an archaeologist digging for the bones or artifacts of an ancient civilization, would likely first find Jimmy Hoffa's body.

Most of Grace's questions are innocuous and odd, but somewhat humorous. She can be so endearing, but it's when she asks questions about *us* that those entombed skeletons uncover themselves and rise to the surface. I don't know why I'm unable to keep them interred.

I tried to deflect. "So let me ask you the same question. How would you describe our relationship?"

"I asked you first, Lewis. I'm calling your hand."

I took a long pause and slowly shook my head. *I don't see any way out of this.* "It's like when I was in 'Nam, on the river boats."

"How so?"

"It was hours, sometimes days of boredom split up by moments of sheer terror. You just never knew when the next attack was coming, or from where. Like now."

She responded matter-of-factly, "So you're equating my question to an attack?"

"Kind of. Not a frontal attack, mind you. Just coming out of nowhere." I wasn't smiling, and my tone was dark and anxious.

"Interesting," she said, staring at me.

Every time she says that and gives me that stare, I know she's thinking of another question, and each succeeding question gets more intense, more focused.

"Then does my question scare you—terrify you?" she asked.

"No. Not exactly."

"Then what?"

"It's damn annoying. It frustrates the hell out of me."

"I believe what frustrates you is that you know the answer and are afraid to face it." Her tone softened, and she smiled. "You've gotten so much better at opening up, Lewis. I truly mean that. Just answer the question, please, and we can both go to sleep."

Her smile was convincing, and I bought it. I wanted to buy it. It was the same smile that beguiled me the first time we met.

I've learned that Grace was a damn good prosecuting attorney in her life before retirement. It showed at times like this. She used her charm before asking those final piercing questions, which felt like the last thrusts of a dagger into some woefully unprepared witness.

"No. That's not the way it works with you, Grace, and you know it," I said, even more agitated. "You'll have twenty more questions. You always treat me like a hostile witness in these bouts, and I know I won't be excused from the witness chair until you're finished with me. But truth be told, I mostly feel that you're prosecuting some ghosts—not me—and it's not fair."

She didn't directly address my anxiety. Instead, she said, "I promise this time I won't. Answer the question and we can both get some much-needed rest."

"Promise?"

"I promise."

Once again, I was sold like some buyer on a used car lot being told that the car I was about to purchase was only driven to church by a little old lady.

"Fine." *Here it goes.* "Living with you is like residing in a fireworks factory where they allow smoking. It's not *if* there will be an explosion, it's *when*!" The explosion was coming from within me. *This is my previous marriage all over again*, I thought, *always having to prove myself.*

That retort apparently got her attention, because she now sat upright, no longer assuming the pose of a Roman emperor eating grapes and sipping wine. Her dark brown eyes narrowed and focused directly on me. "What are you saying?"

"I'm saying we're combustible, Grace. Your questions are like an open flame around gunpowder."

"Bullshit, Lewis! We're not combustible. You're combustible." She pointed her finger at me, and said as emphatically as she could, "This isn't about me. This is about your ex. Isn't it? Just admit it."

"I'm not admitting to shit, Grace, because that's not true," I groused. "This has absolutely nothing to do with her." But it did. More so, it had everything to do with me believing I wasn't good enough for Grace.

"The hell it doesn't. It's always about her when it comes to us. Talk about living with ghosts!" She rolled her eyes, smirked, and shook her head.

I was losing ground and Grace knew it. She was about to unsheathe that dagger.

"Well, here's what I really mean, Grace," my voice elevating to match her finger pointing. "You ask these off-the-wall questions..."

"Oh. So, questions about our relationship are now off the wall?" she cut in.

"No. You're twisting my words. I mean I just never know when those questions about us are coming, and that's what terrifies me!" What really terrified me was that Grace might believe I'm not worthy of her, and I didn't have the courage to say so. What if I wasn't?

"There you go, Lewis. It's only when I ask those questions about us. Thank you for finally admitting it. And it really doesn't matter when I ask them, does it?" She paused. "DOES IT?"

Grace folded her arms across her chest and looked away. She wasn't fishing for a response. Like any good prosecutor, Grace never asked a question to which she didn't already have the answer.

I took a deep breath, collected my thoughts, and added sullenly, "I've fought one war in my life. I'm not going to fight another one. This relationship, like my marriage, is beginning to resemble Vietnam. Except in 'Nam we used bullets, not words. But the effects are the same: the walking wounded." I sighed deeply, and I said,

"There're only so many conflicts a person can fight, and I want to be done with all of them."

Grace turned her head toward me, her arms still folded. I couldn't decide if the look in her eyes was hurt, anger, or confusion. At that moment, I wasn't sure if I cared. I just wanted the discussion to end.

"What do you mean, Lewis?" Gone was the confidence in her voice.

In hindsight, I did care, because I tried my best to limit the damage of that combustible moment. I gently slid my hand to touch her arm. "Grace, I've learned over the years which battles to fight, and fighting to keep us together is one endeavor I'm more than willing to undertake. I'm not a conscript in this battle. I'm a volunteer. But please, stop treating me like a combatant. Start treating me more as a medic." I just wanted to be someone who stopped the bleeding and saved the patient, but I wasn't sure if the patient was me, her, or us.

I asked her to look at the sign that I'd made which hangs by our bedroom doorway. It reads: "I would rather be crazy with you, than sane without you." Then I leaned into Grace, and said, "Why can't you just accept that I love you—that I'm in love with you—and that I want us to work?"

I could see the corners of her mouth turn upward ever so slightly. Then she spoke. "I suppose I like fireworks, Lewis." She kissed me, and then said, "Now go to sleep, sweetheart. I know I will. It's late." She rolled away from me.

I turned off my light. It was then I realized that this conversation had ended the same way it began—with me in the dark.

14

Kintsugi

"You really shouldn't go back into the house." Dori, always the reassuring voice of reason, was concerned.

"And why not? I still have some things in the house that are mine, and I have the right to collect them."

"This isn't about rights. It's about being smart and not giving them ammunition to use against you. And because your attorney advised against it. With you no longer on the deed, he said they could consider it trespassing. Knowing your brother, he's just crazy enough to press charges." There was no anger in her voice. It was more like trepidation, bordering on fear.

"He only advised against it. He didn't say I shouldn't or couldn't do it."

"It's the same thing and you know it."

"Maybe so, but how will they know when they're in Florida?"

"There's no maybe about it. Besides, I wouldn't put it past him to have the neighbors watch the house and report to him. You know, Ian, you're sounding like a child throwing a tantrum. I don't know why you hired and paid for an attorney if you're not going to follow his advice."

I was one of a triad of owners of the house in which I grew up—the other two being my older brother and his mother. Even though she is our biological mother, I long ago stopped referring to her as *my* mother. I just refer to her by her name—Gertrude. My brother doesn't feel the same way.

She caused the divide when I was born, about three years after my father returned from the battlefields of Europe. Gertrude had raised my brother, Henry, alone for the better part of two years—a year while my father was still in Europe, and another while he was recovering at an Army hospital in Kentucky from a third wound he suffered—this one at the German border, while serving with Patton's Third Army. She insisted that since she bore the burden of raising Henry for the first two years of his life, and my father really had no bond with my brother after his return, that I would be his responsibility. "This one is yours," Gertrude said to my father, matter-of-factly. Like two once-friends kids returning baseball cards.

I've never been sure why she felt that way. It didn't seem natural. None of my friends' parents ever did that—at least as far as I knew. Maybe she was just tired, didn't really want me, or was angry at my father for leaving her, regardless of the circumstances. Nonetheless, it was a responsibility my father gladly and wholeheartedly accepted. I was his son, and my brother was hers. There was never any sense of kinship between me and my brother and his mother. It was like two separate and distinct families living in the same house.

My father would take me everywhere. He would only take Henry if he asked to come along, which wasn't often, or when we went somewhere as a family—like on vacation, or to an Army reunion, or to visit my father's family in Chicago.

When my father drove a delivery truck for a restaurant food service company, he would bring me along if he had to make a weekend emergency delivery. The truck had a manual transmission with a huge shift lever on the floor, and he would let me shift it into gear. At eight years of age, that lever seemed as big as me. He would say, "Ready...go!" and I would push or pull the lever to the proper gear as he depressed the clutch. I had to use both hands and all of my strength. Even if I would grind the gear into place, he would always tell me I did a great job, and tousle my tangled crop of red hair.

He, too, had red, wavy hair—like many of his siblings and family members—and a fair complexion which accented his blue eyes. At six-two, and now in his mid-thirties with the same physique as when he left the Army, he was a strikingly handsome man with movie-star looks, who always drew the gaze of ladies—even if he was with my mother, or they with another man—and even from a few envious men.

The man had a quiet intellect. With only a high school education, he could still finish *The New York Times* Sunday crossword puzzle in about an hour without the aid of a dictionary or thesaurus. Although he was a congenial guy who could make you his friend in an instant with his easy smile and soft-spoken manner, my father was a man of few words and fewer nuances, who always kept his own counsel. When he spoke, there was no ambiguity. You listened.

One event still stands out. He took me by train to Philadelphia at a time when there was still passenger train service from our small town. He didn't ask my brother to come along. Other than my trips to Chicago—which were cloistered visits to see my uncles, aunts and cousins—it was my first trip to a big city with my father as a personal guide. He stopped a policeman to ask directions to a museum. The officer had a blasé demeanor and didn't look approachable—until my father addressed him. Each instantly recognized the other had been in the war, and they began to chat.

"Ninety-Fifth Infantry Division. The Iron Men of Metz. Patton's Third," my father proudly stated.

"The Big Red One," the officer responded with equal pride, standing almost at attention.

"We fought and slept in the same mud and dirt," my father said somberly.

"You bet we did, and we lived to tell about it. What can I do for you, soldier?"

"My son and I need directions. Can you help?"

The officer listened, then took out his notepad and wrote down the directions to the museum, and even suggested a few other sites of interest. My father introduced me to the officer, who shook my hand. After a few more minutes' talking, they shook hands and slapped each other's shoulders as they said goodbye, as if they were long-time friends. I suppose in a way, they were. I swear if the officer had been allowed to do so, he would have used his police car as a taxi for us. My father was that good, too, and it wasn't a front. He was genuine; the real deal. The best natural salesperson I have ever met.

My fondest memories, however, were of when I helped my father cook. He didn't get the opportunity all that often with his work schedule, but how he enjoyed it when he did. The TV shows of the day portrayed a mother who stayed at home and prepared meals, and a family who sat for dinner in the dining room at a set time every day. This most definitely was not our home.

Gertrude owned a woman's dress shop, and my father—before he finally landed a job with the post office and had a predictable schedule—rarely sat for meals with the rest of his family. He usually ate alone late at night, most times after his family was already in bed which, in retrospect, still saddens me. Perhaps that's why I still would rather not eat than eat alone. But when he was able to do so, mostly on the weekends, he did the cooking. My brother and I were thankful, as Gertrude really had no desire, nor talent, for cooking. To this day, I do not eat at any place that advertises meals: *Like Mother used to make.*

One of my father's favorite pieces of cooking equipment was a big blue-glazed ceramic mixing bowl. I don't know where he bought it, but I always assumed it was secondhand—probably a throwaway from one of his restaurant customers—being it already showed wear, with numerous chips around the edges which exposed the white ceramic. Not good enough for a diner or restaurant, but more than good enough for our eating establishment.

He would always invite me to help him mix the ingredients du jour. We would both get our hands into the bowl—my small hands squeezing around his large hands—and enjoy feeling the texture of the mix. We didn't talk much. We didn't have to. Our smiles said it all.

"So…let me understand this. You want to sneak back into a house which you couldn't wait to leave and even went so far as to have your name removed from the deed, all at the risk of being charged with trespassing, to retrieve an old mixing bowl. Did I get it right, Ian?"

Her tone started out sarcastically, morphed into incredulity, and ended with her being totally pissed off. I was relieved she was on the other end of the phone.

"It's not just some old mixing bowl. It was my father's, and now it sits in the dark, behind a cupboard door, over a stove, in an empty house." I was passionate in my defense and could hear my voice rise. But it wasn't anger I was feeling. All I could think about was how my father came home late at night, and ate his dinner alone at the kitchen table by the dim solitary light that was built into the range hood, while the rest of us were comfortably asleep. Not once did I get out of bed to join him, or ask how his day went. Now I felt ashamed for being so selfish. All he ever wanted to do was make a little boy—his son—smile, and asked for nothing in return. Now that bowl was alone, and this was my opportunity to redeem myself; to make sure it never again sat in the dark alone. "I won't let it happen again, Dori."

"Let what happen again?" she asked, her tone becoming decidedly softer.

"Never mind. You wouldn't understand. I'm going to get it."

"Okay, Ian. But think about this. What if your brother makes an unannounced visit to the house and is standing there when you walk in? Do you have any idea what will happen next? Do you even care?"

I remained silent, and she filled the void.

"All hell will break loose, Ian. He's crazy enough to have you arrested." Her voice was starting to crack with tears.

"I'm not afraid of Hell, Dori. I've been there enough times in my life and made it through without the Devil even knowing I was there," I said, trying to make light of the situation. "Besides, it wouldn't be the first time I was arrested."

Her voice rose in anger: "You were a teenager then—a juvenile, goddamnit. Can't you see the difference? Now you're an adult where you can't hide behind your age. You'll have a real adult record."

"You're making more of this than it is, sweetheart. Nothing like that will remotely happen. I'll be in and out before anyone knows I was even there."

There was a very long pause. "Dori...? Are you still there?"

"Fine, Ian. Do what the fuck you want," she said between full sobs. "You always do." She hung up.

It was true what she said. All of it. Around the age of ten my maternal grandfather, a bookie, started to mentor me. He had no beef with the way my father was raising me, other than he thought I was growing up too soft. The two got along because he respected my father for his service in the war. My grandfather had fought with the British in WWI after emigrating from Czarist Russia and he, like my father, was a man of few words who always kept his own counsel. He thought of my father as more of a son, than Gertrude as a daughter, and made that known to both at every opportunity.

My grandfather taught me how to fight: how to survive on the streets by using my wits and my fists. At ten he also taught me and my best friend, Mikey, how to run numbers without getting caught. By the age of sixteen, Mikey and I were his collection agency. But it was my fighting and truancy which brought me into direct contact with the police on almost a daily basis.

My father didn't like what I was doing; he had bigger plans and dreams for me, and tried to reason with me and my grandfather. I would just retort by saying I would be okay, that nothing bad would happen to me. My grandfather—who stood an inch taller than my father—would smile, put his hand on my father's right shoulder, and respond to him in his fading Russian accent, "Larry...I love the boy, your son, and I would never let anything bad happen to him. He's a good boy. He just needs to learn the ways of the world. You and your brothers did that growing up on the streets of Chicago, and you turned out to be a good man. So will he."

Except I didn't, and my father reacted. There were several

incidents, at different intersections in our lives, and all had a profound and defining effect on the relationship between us. The first was when I was about fifteen. My father was now working for the post office and was able to sit with his family for dinner. Dinner, when made by my father, was one of the few times I would join him and Gertrude. This time, Henry was home from college for the weekend and we sat and ate as a family: my mother and Henry on one side of the table, and my father and I on the other. I sat to my father's right.

That night I wasn't particularly hungry. I was in a hurry because I needed to attend to my errands, as my grandfather euphemistically referred to his illegal dealings. I finished only about half of my meal, then stood up. My father, without even looking at me, said in his firm but quiet way, "Sit down and finish your dinner, Ian. You're not excused."

"I'm not hungry, Dad, and I have some things to do. Thanks for the dinner."

"I said sit down. I won't tell you again."

I sat back down, and then my mother chimed in with her two cents. "There are children in China who are starving, and they would love a meal like this."

I was, and probably still am but to a lesser degree, a consummate smart-ass. I said, "Then send my meal to them."

The back of my father's right hand caught me squarely across my nose and sent me flying backward off my chair onto the floor. I had been hit in the face many times in fights, but I was always prepared. No hit to the face, before or after my father's, ever caught me more by surprise, or caused such shock. He never struck Henry or me—ever. That task was always left to my mother, who prosecuted that endeavor with great skill and sadistic satisfaction. Henry sat there transfixed, utterly speechless at what had just happened. I have never

It's Always My Fault

asked him, but I have no doubt he felt some smug pleasure that his father's golden boy had just been knocked on his ass—by his patron saint, no less.

My father turned slightly and raised himself from his seat, reached out his hand to me—which I took—and pulled me up from the floor. He handed me a napkin to wipe the blood from my nose. He then grabbed the chair and stood it upright. I was still reeling from the hit as my mother rushed over and ushered me to the sink. There, she soaked the napkin in cold water and directed me to hold it over my nose with my held tilted backward. I saw her shoot a sharp stare toward my father, but he wasn't looking. He kept his head down and continued eating as if nothing had happened. It was then that the tug of war over to whom I held allegiance began.

My mother calmly said, "Ian, go to your room and lie down until the bleeding stops. You can finish your dinner later."

"He'll finish his dinner now, Gertrude," my father said without looking up. "There's only one dinnertime, and this is it. Ian, sit down and finish your dinner."

There was a pause, a very long pause, to see which master I would serve. They were two people calling the same dog, waiting to see which one the dog would run to. I sat down.

My father looked at me and, with an even, low tone, spoke: "Don't you ever speak to your mother in that manner again. Ever."

He continued eating. I didn't respond, because no response was necessary. Both Gertrude and I had our answers. She and my father may not have had the most loving of relationships, but there was still a strong sense of generational honor—and Gertrude was still his wife.

My father and I never spoke of that incident until almost twenty years later—a year before he passed away—when I came to visit. I was sitting next to him on the couch, both of us watching a ball game. His hair had faded to auburn with streaks of gray, but his mustache remained fiery red. He was still a handsome guy. As much as I enjoyed being with him, I wasn't smiling this time. He had a sixth sense that I wanted to say something. My father picked up the remote, pointed it at the TV to turn it off, and lit up another Lucky Strike.

"What's on your mind, Ian?"

I thought about playing stupid and just saying "Nothing." But I knew he wouldn't believe it. Besides, the man deserved the truth, especially after all the hell I put him through when I was younger. "Do you remember when you hit me at the dinner table?"

He took a drag on his cigarette. "Yes, I remember. What about it?"

"Well…I just wanted to say that I'm sorry for the way I behaved and spoke to Mom, that's all." I was hoping for an apology in return—something that would show me how he felt about striking me.

Instead he put down his cigarette, looked straight into my eyes, and said, "It took you long enough, but that apology is owed to your mother, not me." With that said he turned away, picked up his cigarette, and clicked the TV back on. I should already have known how he felt, because of a discussion I overheard about fifteen years earlier. I just wasn't as smart or insightful as I thought, and didn't connect the dots.

The summer after I turned eighteen I was arrested for stealing a car. It wasn't the first car I stole, nor was it the first time I disappointed my father, but it was the first as an adult rather than a juvenile. The judge gave me a choice of either four years in the military—at the height of the Vietnam War no less—or four years in the county prison. If I served honorably, my record would be expunged. If I went to prison, I would have a record forever. What a choice—either possibly dying in Vietnam, or living with a record. Both my father and grandfather—for whom I decided to no longer work, after an irate customer, during one of our collections, caught me in the head with a bat, causing a two-inch gash which required a dozen or so stitches—convinced me the military was the better of two evils. I joined the Navy.

Before I acted on that decision, I came home earlier than usual for one of my father's weekend dinners. I was always hungry. Running numbers, fighting and collecting bad debts from deadbeat customers will do that. My parents were in the kitchen and didn't hear me come in. I could barely make out the conversation as they were talking softly, but something told me it was one which I didn't want to walk into. I stayed in the dining room, but still in earshot for the last part of the exchange.

"When are you going to get rid of the blue mixing bowl, Larry? It's so chipped, and it's not like we can't afford a better one. And speaking of damaged goods," my mother sanctimoniously stated, "I can't wait for Ian to leave. Perhaps then we'll have some peace knowing that the next knock on the door won't be the police."

I peeked around the corner and saw my father turn toward my mother to address her question: "You're right, Gertrude. This bowl is a piece of shit. But even damaged goods still have value and purpose." His response was a culmination of all the death and misery he had seen and experienced in his life. Silence from my mother. My father had made his point, but I didn't make the connection.

He reinforced those feelings later when he was the only one to write or visit me, while I was recuperating for four months in a Hawaiian hospital from wounds I suffered in 'Nam. My river boat was the sole target of an ambush while on a classified mission with two other boats. I was the only survivor. Not one call, letter, or visit from Gertrude or Henry; just my father. And yet, I still didn't get it. God was I dense.

It wasn't until some five years after his death that I told my mother, in one of our rare civil conversations, that I had apologized to my father. I then, finally and formally, apologized to her for my comment. She thanked me, but what she said next was yet another bat to my head. "I never saw your father cry, but he cried that night in bed. Your father never forgave himself for hitting you, Ian. As you know, your father was a man of few words, much to my chagrin. But I cannot tell you how many times, right up until his death, for no apparent reason at all, he would blurt out: 'I should never have lost my temper and hit him, Gertrude. He didn't deserve to be treated that way.' Through all of the disappointments and heartaches, he always loved you, Ian. Always." This time…this time, I finally got it. But I didn't feel relieved or vindicated. I felt repentant.

Given the nature of my relationship with Gertrude, I have often wondered if she told me to assuage my torment, or to add salt to that open wound. I would like to think it was the former, but believe it was the latter.

A few days after that last stormy conversation with Dori—in spite of her protests, in spite of my attorney's advice—I stopped at the old house. It was night, and there was a single light on in the living room. I walked straight to the kitchen, also illuminated, but only by the light under the range hood. I stopped for a moment, fully expecting to see my father eating his dinner. *That should never have happened*, I thought.

Over the stove, behind the cupboard door, sat the blue bowl. I needed something in which to carry it—something inconspicuous. I spotted a large brown bag—the kind the grocery stores still offer as a choice between paper or plastic—and promptly put the bowl into it. Then I threw in a couple of other items and quickly left, hoping none of the spying neighbors had ratted me out to my brother or the police. Driving to my new apartment I felt relief and satisfaction—like someone who just rescued a hostage without being spotted or apprehended.

I parked the car and opened the passenger door to retrieve my backpack and the brown bag lying on the front seat. After slinging the backpack over my left shoulder, I grabbed the bag with my right hand. That blue bowl, that old blue bowl with the weight of all of its memories, was too much for the bag. Before I could place it on the ground so I could shut the door, there was a tear, a clumsy attempt to grab the bag, and then a sickening crack as it hit the sidewalk. I wasn't sure if the sound came from my heart or the bowl. I stood there for a few moments in somber shock, trying to comprehend what had just happened. Then I cradled the bag, now full of my shattered plans, in my arms and raced up the stairs to my second-floor apartment, as if it were a dying patient I was attempting to get into the emergency room before it expired.

Five pieces. All clean breaks. I spread out a dish towel and carefully placed the pieces on it. I stared at it, willing it to heal itself. *What have I done?*

I walked to the den, sat down in my lounger, lit a cigarette. It was about the time I usually called Dori, but we hadn't spoken, or even texted each other, since that last tearful call two days earlier. *Do I tell her what really happened, or just put on a happy face and say nothing?* I decided I had to tell her the truth. She would find out sooner rather than later. Besides, Dori had become my confidante, and I didn't want the relationship to be encumbered by lies or omissions of the truth. I had to walk into that minefield.

"Hi, Ian. Funny you should call."

"Why's that?"

"Because I was about to call you. I wanted to apologize for the way I went off on you during the last call."

"No apology necessary, sweetheart. Everything you said was true. I'm sorry I was such a rock head. But thanks just the same."

"How was your day?"

"Work was fine, but I need to tell you what happened after work." Stepping into the unknown, I recounted all of it. "I never should have put the bowl on the bottom of the bag. That was stupid."

I hoped to garner some sympathy. Instead, there was dead silence on Dori's end. I was now in the center of that field of explosives, and saw no clear path by which to extricate myself safely. When Dori finally spoke, the whole field started to explode around me. She made no attempt to hide her anger.

"No, Ian… No. Stupid was you entering the house. The bowl didn't break because of your stupidity. It broke because of your arrogance."

"What the hell is that supposed to mean?"

"It means just what I said, you arrogant, selfish, son of a bitch. All you thought of was yourself. You really didn't give a shit about the bowl, or you would have taken better care to make sure it was protected. And you certainly didn't consider my feelings. You just wanted to stick your finger in your brother's and mother's collective eye to say, 'See? I can enter the house when I damn well feel like it and take what I want.'"

"That's not—"

"Shut the hell up, Ian. I'm not through."

I felt like I was back in 'Nam, in the middle of a horrific firefight with no ammunition. That minefield was tearing me apart. *Why on earth did I ever enter it?*

"I'll give you credit, Ian. You've been in some tough spots in your life and always managed to come through on the plus side. But that didn't make you stronger, or more humble, confident, or thankful. It made you cynical and arrogant. What is it you always said? 'I've done so much, with so little, for so long, that I now believe I can do the impossible with absolutely nothing, forever.' I used to think that was cute and clever, and, in some way, I admired you for your strength of character and tenacity. Now I see it for what it really is, for what you really are—a spoiled, arrogant child who can't stand to have things not go his way. I know you had to repeat that mantra to keep you going, but you've said that bullshit line for so long, you actually started to believe it! And that's what really scares the shit out of me."

The tears started to come through the phone again. "I thought I was starting to really know you. But I now realize that's not possible, because you don't even know yourself. Knowing you is like attempting to put your arms around fog. Get a grip, Ian. And when you can admit what you've really become, then maybe, just maybe, you and I can have a relationship that's built on something more stable than delusions of grandeur. I gotta go." She hung up.

Dori was right...again. I still wasn't connecting the dots. Had the bowl meant that much to me, I not only would have taken greater care when I transported it, I would have taken it when I moved. But the bowl did have meaning to me; it connected me to my father—the one parent who loved me unconditionally. I did the right thing, but for the wrong reason. It wasn't the first time.

I volunteered—yes volunteered—for combat duty in Vietnam, even though I had already graduated from submarine school and was attending the Navy's advanced communication courses. And not for some patriotic reason, but because Mikey—my best friend and accomplice in my youthful, nefarious enterprises—who enlisted as a Marine, was killed halfway through his Vietnam tour. I wanted to avenge his death. After I recovered from my wounds, I served five more years on submarines. Again, not because I wanted to serve my country or because I had a great love of working in the depths of the sea, but because I was doing something most people didn't have the balls to do. It also gave me the time I needed to hide from the world and recover emotionally from 'Nam.

The right things, for the wrong reasons. The story of my life. Dori knew what I had done, but she didn't know why I had done them. She was on the cusp of understanding it all, and that scared the hell out of me.

Several days after that last call from Dori, I confided to a friend at work all that had gone down. Within earshot was a young girl working part-time while she attended graduate school. Though she had been there about a week, I had never made the attempt to introduce myself—a hangover habit from my days in the Navy, especially Vietnam.

While on a smoke break a couple of days later, she came over and introduced herself, and asked if we could talk. I was expecting her to ask me about work and how she could do her job better. Instead, she hesitated for a moment and then sheepishly said, "I overheard your conversation with Alex."

I stared at her and remained silent, not knowing where this conversation was going. She continued, "I studied in Japan during my junior year in college, and became fascinated by the people, their history and culture. My graduate work is an extension of that experience."

"That's interesting, Bailey, and I wish you well in your studies. But what does any of that have to do with me?"

Bailey responded timidly, hearing the less-than-enthusiastic tone of my voice: "I believe I have a solution for your bowl."

"How's that?"

"Have you ever heard of *kintsugi*?"

"No. What is it?"

"It's the Japanese art of fixing broken pottery with lacquer mixed with powdered gold, silver, or platinum."

"Terrific. Let me know where I can get my hands on some of those materials. For me, it's going to be super glue."

"But people use glue to hide the damage."

"Precisely. Who wants to see the cracks?"

Bailey explained, "The philosophy behind kintsugi treats breakage and repair as part of the history of an object—something to celebrate, rather than something to disguise. An art form, if you like. The life of an object is extended by transforming it, rather than allowing its service to end just because it's become damaged goods."

Damaged goods. That caught my full attention. Perhaps my father was using kintsugi intuitively: attempting to extend my life by transforming me into someone of value and purpose—not by disguising my flaws, but by having me recognize them, and understand that they, too, are a part of my history.

"Thanks for the advice, Bailey. I'll give it serious consideration. Really."

"You're welcome. The bowl apparently means a great deal to you, and it deserves a better place than stuck away in a cupboard to be forgotten. I may be going out on a limb, Ian, but my guess is the bowl isn't the only thing you want to repair."

I could feel a small smile form on my face. "You're a smart, intuitive young lady and wise beyond your years." I paused briefly then said, "We should be getting back in before they start to miss us."

As we reached the door to our office, I stopped and turned to Bailey. "I apologize for not introducing myself earlier. Just an old, outdated, and stupid habit. I'm delighted we had the chance to chat."

Several months after I moved into my apartment, I was finally unpacked and had my new place furnished and decorated. It was time to open the doors to my friends for an inaugural dinner. The apartment was ideal. I occupied the second and third floors of a completely renovated and refurbished three-story Victorian mansion located in what they now call The Historic District of the city. It had all the room and amenities I ever wanted. More so, it was the first place I could really call home since my divorce years earlier.

The apartment wasn't the only thing that went through transformation. Bailey's comment continued to gnaw at me like a river slowly, relentlessly, carving out a canyon. I still believed in my mantra, and came to the conclusion there was absolutely no reason I couldn't transform myself. My life, my relationship with my friends and my children—and especially with Dori—depended upon it, now. I didn't have the luxury of several thousand years. My relationship with Henry and Gertrude? Well...that would have to wait for another epiphany.

After about an hour of socializing, I ushered everyone into the dining room, which I had kept hidden behind closed doors until that moment. The spacious room with its ornate, but tasteful, woodwork was the crown jewel of the apartment. Its high ceiling was adorned by a Victorian-style chandelier in the center. Under it sat a period-appropriate cherry dining room set I found at an estate sale, which rested regally on a lush, pale oriental rug with a simple, graceful, multi-color design. The centerpiece of the room was a stately fireplace bound in exquisitely carved mahogany, capped with two mantels which framed a mirror.

As the guests were about to be seated, Suzanne—the better half of a couple I had known since before my divorce—looked at the mantel above the mirror and said with childlike wonderment, "This blue bowl, Ian. It's so unique and beautiful. Simply elegant. I have never seen a piece of pottery decorated in such fashion. Where on earth did you find it?"

I glanced over at Dori, who gave me her crooked smile, and nodded her head, as if to say: "Go ahead, Ian. Tell the story. You've earned it."

I put my drink down and pushed my hands into the pockets of my pants—a tell of mine since I was a kid, when I was about to share some secret. I glanced down reflectively, then raised my head and smiled at Suzanne. "Have you ever heard of kintsugi?"

Some of the stories in this anthology were first published in literary journals (both online media and print media), giving the below-named publications either first North American serial rights or onetime electronic rights (first rights for an established period of time). The stories are listed according to their corresponding dates of publication, in chronological order from earliest to most recent, as of the date of this anthology. The author is grateful to the editors of these journals for their vision and confidence.

Solomon's Shadow, *Red Fez,* February 2015

The Box, *Remarkable Doorways Online Literary Magazine,* May 2015

Kintsugi, *The Writing Disorder,* June 2015

Where's the Cow?, *Indiana Voice Journal,* January 2016

Wooden Statements, *The Furious Gazelle*, December 2015

As If, *Slippery Elm*, January 2016

Driving Lessons, *Pour Vida Zine*, Winter 2016

Done with Crazy, *Potluck Mag,* April 2016

Separated at Birth, *Cobalt Review* (print), May 2016

Benjamin Stahlman, Scholar, *Evening Press Review* (print), April/May 2017

It's Always My Fault, *Indian Review*, September 2016

Combustible, *Philadelphia Stories*, (print) June 2017

It Happened Over Coffee...and a Bagel, *Evening Street Press*, August 2018